High Dive

High Dive

Tammar Stein

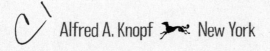

Alfred A. Knopf ✶ New York

THIS IS A BORZOI BOOK PUBLISHED BY ALFRED A. KNOPF

Published in the United States by Alfred A. Knopf, an imprint of Random House Children's
Books, a division of Random House, Inc., New York.

Knopf, Borzoi Books, and the colophon are registered trademarks of Random House, Inc.

Visit us on the Web! www.randomhouse.com/teens

Educators and librarians, for a variety of teaching tools,
visit us at www.randomhouse.com/teachers

Library of Congress Cataloging-in-Publication Data
Stein, Tammar.
High dive / Tammar Stein. — 1st ed.
      p. cm.
Summary: With her mother stationed in Iraq as an Army nurse, Vanderbilt University student
Arden Vogel, whose father was killed in a traffic accident a few years earlier, impulsively ends up
on a tour of Europe with a group of college girls she meets on her way to attend to some family
business in Sardinia.
ISBN 978-0-375-83024-2 (trade) — ISBN 978-0-375-93024-9 (lib. bdg.)
[1. Vacations—Fiction. 2. Single parent families—Fiction. 3. Loss (Psychology)—Fiction.
4. Friendship—Fiction. 5. Europe—Fiction. 6. Iraq War, 2003—Fiction.] I. Title.
PZ7.S821645Hi 2008
[Fic]—dc22
2007049657

The text of this book is set in 11-point Goudy.

Printed in the United States of America
June 2008
10 9 8 7 6 5 4 3 2 1
First Edition

To my parents—who always encouraged me
to go off on adventures

1.

The phone rang at 6 a.m. Even though I expected it, my heart leapt at the shrill sound. I lunged for the receiver, picking it up before the ring ended, and looked over at my roommate. She'd burrowed deeper undercover. I could see only a skein of hair on the pillow. Good.

I glanced at the clock to begin the countdown. My mom and I had exactly fifteen minutes for the phone call.

Technically, everyone was allowed two fifteen-minute DSN, the military phone system, calls a week, but we rarely managed two. Usually it was one call, which you might think meant we could talk for thirty minutes, but the army doesn't work that way.

"Hi, sweetie," my mom said. Sometimes the connection was clear; other times it crackled and buzzed, her voice fading in and out. We had a good connection this time. I closed my eyes at the sound of her voice, trying to breathe it in, trying to soak in it. "How are you?"

I spent three minutes telling her about a paper I'd turned in

1

and an upcoming final that worried me. "How are you doing?" I asked. I couldn't skip that even though I knew she wouldn't tell me anything important.

"It's 120 degrees today," she said. "Don't believe what people say about 'dry heat.' It's like stepping into an oven. And summer's just starting. Just another beautiful day in Baghdad. Oh, and yesterday we had a sandstorm."

"Was it as bad as everyone said it would be?" A deployment to Iraq sucked on many levels. For my mom, the weather was high on the list.

"It was worse. The sky turned orange. It was like the thickest fog you've ever seen, like a fine misty rain, but it was sand." I winced. "The sand whipped so hard even the birds couldn't fly."

I glanced at the clock. Five minutes down. Ten to go. And I hadn't brought up the trip to Sardinia.

Two months ago an Italian real estate agent contacted my mom about selling our vacation house in Sardinia. It took a few weeks before my mom had told me. I think she worried about my feelings, but I didn't blame her for wanting to sell.

"When we bought the place, Dad and I joked we'd retire there," she had said. That was during a phone call five weeks ago, when she finally filled me in. "That's not going to happen now, is it?"

"Plus, the roof's going to go any day now," she'd said, going on. Her voice had dropped out, then came back. "The plumbing all needs to be replaced."

I'd grown up on the story of how my parents bought the little house on their honeymoon. They knew my mom's military career would keep them moving a lot. A permanent place, they reasoned, even a vacation home they'd visit only once a year, was like having a real home.

"It's okay, Mom. It makes sense."

"I can't believe those people are offering so much money for such a dump," she'd said, trying to laugh.

"It's not a dump." I couldn't help defending the house. But it was a lot of money, enough to give my mom a comfortable nest egg when she finally left the army.

"You've always loved it best. We can keep it if you want," she had said in a rush. Because of the delay, her reply and mine came on top of each other.

Silence again. I wasn't sure if she'd heard me. But there wasn't time to get into long discussions. There were too many other important things to worry about.

"No, it makes sense to sell it," I'd said, pragmatic and practical. I ignored the deep pang that said I was turning my back on the place of my best memories, my favorite vacations, the promise my dad made to me every year if I was good.

I managed to convince her that since I already had a ticket to visit her in Germany—I'd purchased it before we knew she'd be deployed—I'd use my ticket and make my way down to Sardinia to close up the house. She didn't interrupt me much. Partly because it was easier to let one person talk instead of having a conversation full of time delays and dead air, and partly because I was saying everything she needed to hear.

I didn't lie to my mom when I had told her I wanted to do it; it was just that I hadn't really thought it through.

Then last week, as school was winding down and my trip was coming up, it finally occurred to me it might be really awful to go to Sardinia alone.

I had less than ten minutes to try and explain.

"So about the house," I said now, keeping an eye on the roommate and on the clock.

"I worry about you going to Sardinia alone," she said, echoing my thoughts. "Are you sure you want to do this?"

With a sinking heart, I realized that I couldn't burden her with my doubts. She'd been in Iraq for five months; I couldn't tell her that I was scared to go alone. That the beach house in Sardinia was the closest thing I had to a childhood home and I didn't want to be the one to turn off the lights and lock the door.

"Really, Mom, it's no problem."

"You'll be so lonely there. And how will you manage without a car?"

Perhaps she had also agreed to my offer without fully thinking it through. But I couldn't back down now. I volunteered to close the house to take one worry off her shoulders. I wasn't about to put it back on.

"Yeah, it's such a hardship to go spend a couple of weeks at a beach house in Sardinia. Honestly, Mom, it'll be awesome to travel to Europe. Hang out at the beach, eat great food. All my friends are so jealous."

Five minutes left.

"This will be a great way to say goodbye to the old place," I said. "It'll give me closure."

"Closure, huh?" my mom said.

I laughed at her tone. "I'll mail you biscotti and Baci," I offered.

"Now you're talking."

I tried not to think about how far away she was, how small and miserable her quarters were. How dangerous Iraq was. How much I missed her.

"Stay safe," I told her, suddenly fighting tears.

"I will, sweetheart," she said gently. "You make me proud."

One minute to go.

Anything I didn't take away during this last visit would be sold with the house. Chances were the new owners would throw everything out because they were rich and fancy and the furniture was old and didn't hold any memories for them. I tried not to let that bother me, but it did. Oh, it did.

"Stay safe, Mom," I said again, as if saying it enough could make it happen. "I love you."

Our time was up.

2.

Three weeks later, I was on a plane heading east. My bag was a carry-on, my return date in a month. I was entirely flexible; all I needed was a bit of courage to change my plans. Cruising in the air at thirty-three thousand feet, I decided that for once I wasn't going to do everything I was supposed to.

It was the three college girls sitting near me on the flight that got me thinking. Their bags were full of candy, guidebooks, scented lotions, and screaming red lipstick. My bag had a small first aid kit, an international phone card, and duplicate photocopies of my passport and credit card so that if they were stolen, I wouldn't be stranded. Somehow, it seemed like they were ready for a good time and I wasn't.

Thirty minutes into the flight, we were exchanging all sorts of personal information. I even told one of the girls, Katie, that my mom was deployed in Iraq, which wasn't something that I usually told strangers.

"My boyfriend's in ROTC," Katie told me as soon as she found out I was an army brat.

"Really?" I asked, immediately inclined to like her better. "What branch?"

"Army."

"Best there is," I said, even though I didn't quite believe that. "It's true what they say, you know—join the military, see the world. I've lived in three countries and four states, including Texas."

That pleased her.

"Best there is," she parroted.

"Don't mess with Texas," Lola, the heavy one with the beautiful hair, said, overhearing our conversation.

"What? Did I hear someone say something bad about Texas? Let me at 'em," growled Madison, looking ridiculous in spiky pigtails.

"I like Texas," I said, holding my hands up in surrender. "I lived there during junior high. It was great."

"I knew there was a reason we liked you," Lola said. "You're practically a Texan yourself."

Then our dinner came and we groaned at the rock-hard roll, the limp salad, and the tiny serving of pasta.

Hours later, when Madison had fallen asleep and Lola was listening to her iPod, her eyes glazed over in a tired trance, Katie showed me a photo of Jack, her boyfriend.

"I worry about him," she said. "I have nightmares sometimes that he'll be sent to Iraq." She told me this in that quiet in-between time, when we were flying over the endless black Atlantic, with everyone around us asleep, immersed in the feeling of being untethered from space and time. The sun was starting to glow at the horizon even though my internal clock insisted it was the middle of the night.

"It happens. My mom's there right now."

When I first found out about the deployment, I'd tell people my mom was heading to Iraq. I expected them to be impressed. But instead, they'd give me the same look I might give someone if they told me they had been diagnosed with cancer. Concern, pity, and that slight hint of distaste. They looked at me like something awful was about to happen to my mom. Like something awful had already happened.

I hated that look. I hated that foregone conclusion. I didn't need anyone else's bad feelings about this; I had enough of my own.

"I'm sorry," Katie said. "I hope you don't think I was being rude."

"It's okay. It's what everyone thinks."

"How is she? What's it like over there?"

"She's very busy. That's what she mostly e-mails about. My mom's a nurse at a combat support hospital. It's busier than the busiest ER in the States." She worked twelve-hour shifts, six, sometimes seven days a week. It was the reason we only talked once a week: she simply didn't have the time.

"Wow," Katie said.

I told her that about two-thirds of the victims at my mom's hospital were Iraqis. A thirty-year-old mom with shrapnel in her brain, a baby with perforated intestines. My mom was not a pediatric nurse. It was hard, I knew. She wasn't prepared for child patients.

"My mom said to imagine the most difficult patient a stateside ER might see in a day. They see three or four of them a day. And in the States it's mostly blunt trauma, like car accidents, but in Iraq it's mostly penetrating injuries, shrapnel, bullets, things like that." I knew I sounded like a newscaster. But it was hard to describe it.

My mom almost never talked about it. When she did, the word she used was *horrific*. As in: *horrific injuries*. Then a pause. Then, in a quiet voice, just *horrific*. This during one of our fifteen-minute phone calls, toward the end, when there was no time for me to ask more.

"Oh," Katie said again. "That's horrible."

"What can you do." I shrugged, trying to sound tough. I had asked my mom the same questions, of course. *What's it like over there? How's it different?* Especially in the first few months, when the deployment was new. When I was still watching the news, getting sucked into the tabloid-style-news delivery, which left me with more questions than answers. It took me a while to learn to look for my news online.

She usually ducked the question, describing her trailer, the sweet deal where contractors do her laundry and even fold it for free. But I kept tugging at her. *Is it different from what you were doing before? Is it like they show on CNN?* I wanted to know the meat of it. I wanted to know if she would come back different. And the answer was yes. Though she'd deny it. I could feel it in her e-mails, in her words.

A few weeks ago, long after the last time I asked her, she wrote an e-mail, posted before dawn.

You asked me what we do here, how it's different than working in the ICU in the States or in Germany. I don't think I can explain it to you, kiddo. I don't think I have enough words. There was one kid, and I call him a kid because he's younger than you. He woke up with no arms. I sat down next to him and tried to explain. Another woke up crying because he had to shoot a child while on a mission. You sit and talk to them. Well, actually, you listen. You validate their feelings. You try not to cry in front of them, but sometimes you do. Sometimes you leave their room and cry in the hallway.

Later, you wonder what happened to them. Some of them die en route. Many of them just . . . vanish. Some of them volunteer to return as soon as their convalescent leave is over. Even while they're under our care, in massive pain, all they can talk about is returning to their buddies.

I've been a nurse for twenty years. Nothing prepared me for this. I don't know what could. But if I didn't know what I was about, I would say this is the only place for me. There's no place in the world that needs me like the trauma center in Baghdad.

"So . . . you said she lives in a trailer?" Katie said, drawing me out of my trance. "I kind of pictured tents, like from M*A*S*H."

"It might be different in the forward bases, but where my mom is, it's a bunch of trailers. There's this tradition that you try to leave your section of the trailer better for the guy after you. My mom's trailer already had a television and a microwave when she arrived."

"No way." The M*A*S*H image was a hard one to shake.

"Yeah, she's already bought a coffeemaker she's going to leave. And the last time we talked, she bought a bike." It was much easier to talk about this than the rest of it.

"A bike? I can't picture someone riding a bike in Iraq."

I smiled at her tone. It implied a pink bike with a basket and streamers, making its way through a minefield of IEDs.

"The base is pretty big. There are shuttles to take you to the DFAC—that's the dining hall—but they don't have great hours. So . . . bicycles. My mom says when you walk into the PX or the food court, you could be in any mall in America. There's Baskin-Robbins, Popeye's, stuff like that. It's completely surreal. The USO sends people to boost moral. One time my mom walked into the PX after a massive surgery and there were all these professional cheerleaders in their tiny skirts greeting people and signing autographs. Let me tell you, the PX is making a killing over there."

Katie winced at my choice of words.

"You know what I mean," I said, a touch defensive.

"I know, Arden," she said, touching my hand. "I know what you mean."

A few hours later, the Fasten Seat Belt sign chimed on.

Madison, Lola, and Katie had spent the last twenty minutes picking my brain about the must-see places in Germany and the Czech Republic.

When I told Katie, "Write this down—this is the best spa in the Czech Republic," she wrote it down in the margins of her guidebook like a student hoping to ace an exam. She closed the book with a decisive snap, her hand splayed across the cover.

We shared a grin. The thought crossed my mind that I would have much more fun traveling with them than doing what I was supposed to do. As if she shared the thought, Katie grabbed my hand.

"Arden," she said, flicking a quick look at Madison and Lola, who were watching us. "Why don't you skip the next leg to Germany? Come stay in Paris with us."

I hadn't been in Paris for nearly nine years. For an instant, I had that same slightly queasy feeling I get whenever I stand at the edge of a diving board. Where my toes curl around the edge of the board and the water seems impossibly far away. Where a part of me wants to turn around and climb back down the ladder.

The two girls, kneeling on their seats and facing us like two gophers, exchanged a swift look at this offer, then turned to me with matching excited smiles.

The plane started a slow descent. The flaps on the wings came down. The constant engine hum that had been with us for the past eight hours changed its pitch.

"You should do that. It would be so awesome!"

"That would rock, Arden."

Their tone seemed sincere, their excitement, their energy contagious.

I had twenty minutes until the plane landed in Paris. From there, I had a connecting flight to take me to Germany. It had been a year since I'd been there, since I'd started college.

From Heidelberg, I was supposed to travel to Italy and close up our house in Sardinia.

"Sure," I told them, these almost-perfect strangers. "I'll join you." Because in the end, no matter how scared I got, I always jumped off the high dive.

They shrieked and clapped and woke up the few passengers near us who'd managed to stay asleep through the pilot's landing announcement.

I looked out the window, past my own reflection, at the blinking red light on the wing.

I wasn't tired. I wasn't hungry. I didn't know what to name the restless, uncomfortable feeling inside me. There was no point in thinking about the house, no point in worrying about my mother. No point in missing my dad.

Don't borrow trouble, my mom always said. But this time, I did.

3.

When we landed at Charles de Gaulle, I ushered them from the gate to passport control to baggage claim. When Lola wanted a taxi to get downtown, I explained it was cheaper and faster to take the RER, a Paris subway. I found the kiosk and bought four tickets since none of them had any euros.

"Don't worry about it," I said when they tried to figure out how much they owed me in dollars. "Just pay me back when you get euros." It cost over seventeen dollars a ticket. As I told them to pay me back later, I realized there was a decent chance I wouldn't see the money again.

We passed the twenty-minute ride in silence, settling into a rocking motion, and I tried not to fall asleep. There was something about trains and subways that was always soporific. But I fought the urge to doze because I knew none of the others would know when to get off.

The Gare du Nord, the main train station in Paris, was loud and busy with smells of warm croissants and urine vying for attention. There were large banner ads in French, and the commuters around us spoke it with an unaffected elegance.

"This is Paris! I can't believe it—I'm going to faint." Lola spread her arms way out, spinning on the platform. She laughed out loud, a full belly laugh that made people smile even as they dodged her outspread arms.

Madison, her tiny nose stud catching the light, kept crooning, *"I love Paris in the springtime. . . . I love Paris in the fall. . . ."*

I loved how excited they were, like they'd reached Oz or Narnia instead of a Paris subway that was dank and damp. I joined them because I craved this, this easy and natural happiness, this giddiness for life.

When was the last time I was excited like that?

That was easy. When my mom told us she got the transfer to Germany. Three years ago, but it felt like thirty.

"Should you call your mom to let her know you changed your plans?" Katie asked, as if reading my mind.

There wasn't a way to call my mom.

I had my routine at school. I checked my e-mail first thing in the morning. I always had a morning e-mail from her. I had my cell phone with me, charged and set on vibrate, even though school policy said phones must be turned off during class. No one had the number but my mom, my roommate, and the dean of students. It was a phone for bad news. If it rang, then either my mom was injured or someone was calling to tell me there were guys in uniform looking for me. My mom always called my room phone during her allotted phone time, never my cell. My cell phone was for emergencies only. It was never off and never far from me.

Now, for a whole month, I wouldn't have it. It wasn't compatible with the European cell phone system. The only way I had to stay in touch with my mom for the month was e-mail. It made me a little nervous, but in a weird way, it was nice. It was completely irrational, but I didn't have to worry about the phone ringing with bad news. As if that changed anything.

"I'll e-mail her," I said. "As soon as we get settled. It should be easy to find an Internet café."

"Awesome. I'll come with you," she said. "I know my family would love to hear from me too."

With Katie's open guidebook and all our packs on the floor, we stood out as tourists. When my family had traveled, my dad always made sure we didn't stand out in the open to read a map, didn't carry cameras slung around our necks. Little things to keep us from standing out as tourists. I didn't like sticking out, but I quickly saw half a dozen others just like us. Still, I kept an eye on the various people who hurried past us, making sure no one tried to slip a hand into a pocket and relieve us of our wallets or ease away with one of our purses.

"Where are you guys staying tonight?" I asked while we waited. It was sinking in that I skipped my flight to Germany, and I couldn't believe I'd done something so bold, so impulsive and inexplicable. No one in the whole world knew where I was right now except for three girls I'd met a few hours ago. I had the sense of how easy it was to disappear. With a puff of air, I could dissolve.

"There's this great hostel," Katie said. "It's only twenty bucks a night and it's right in the Latin Quarter. My roommate's French TA told her about it. In the summer, anyone under twenty-five can stay there."

"That sounds great," I said. Paris hotels were notoriously expensive and didn't give you a lot for your money. I remembered from my last visit here that my parents couldn't stop complaining about how expensive our tiny, dark room was.

"I have the name and address written here somewhere." She flipped through the guidebook, looking for a piece of paper.

"Great. If you don't mind, I'll call and make a reservation."

"Just come with us. We're going there now."

"Wonderful!" It was an omen, everything falling into place so smoothly. The internal debate that was raging in my head about whether or not joining these girls was incredibly stupid was over. I had a great, cheap place to spend the night; what else was there to worry about?

While we waited for Madison to come back from the restroom, I went to the information kiosk and found when the train to Florence left. From Florence, it'd be easy to get to Genoa and catch the ferry that sailed to Sardinia or catch a flight from Bologna.

I rejoined the girls, feeling on top of things. Now all I needed was to book the hostel for the night and I was set.

"Crap!" Lola's wail drew stares. "I left my camera on the plane!"

"Are you sure? Did you check your backpack?" I asked.

"Of course I did," she moaned. "I just got here. How am I going to take pictures?"

"Are you sure it's not in your luggage?"

"I'm sure. Remember?" she said, a bit sharply. "I pulled it out to take a picture of us when we landed. It was such a great picture too."

Katie hugged Lola in sympathy. I stood and stared, not sure what to say. Did I join in the group hug? Did I walk away to give them space?

Standing awkwardly to the side, I waited for Lola to get over her upset before asking Katie for the address of the hostel, but Madison came back from the restroom before I found the chance.

"They have lockers here. We can check our bags and start sightseeing right away!"

I wanted to cement my night's stay at the hostel. But Katie checked the regulations of the hostel from the notes she had and discovered check-in wasn't until three. Since it was only ten, they wanted to leave our packs at the station and get started with the fun.

"You don't mind, do you?" she asked.

"Places here fill up fast," I said uneasily.

"When I called to confirm our reservations two days ago," Katie said, "they had a bunch of beds available. There's no way they filled up thirty beds in two days. No one knows about this place."

They were buzzing with excitement, ready to see the town. Katie spotted an ATM and everyone withdrew euros. I knew that I should start calling places, but Lola practically danced in place. She and Madison started twirling each other; then they grabbed me and Katie and we were all dancing and spinning in the middle of the station. I never actually decided to let things slide, but the next thing I knew, I let them twirl me along to the lockers.

We checked our bags, paid the fee for the lockers, and hurried toward the bright Paris sun.

"Okay, ladies," I said. "The metro's this way."

They were heading up and out, but the metro was underground and the signs pointed away from the large glass doors.

They obediently changed direction, and while Lola and

Madison tried to figure out the metro ticket-vending machine, Katie and I studied the map to see which line would take us to la Tour Eiffel.

"It doesn't look like there's a direct line," Katie said, half disappointed, half outraged. "Let's just take a taxi."

We piled into a Mercedes and I hung on for dear life in the smoky cab as the driver peeled away from the curb. The French apparently didn't believe in painting lane markers. On a road wide enough for four lanes of traffic, there were sometimes six cars abreast, sometimes two. Our taxi driver darted in and around oncoming traffic as if she were driving a zippy little motorcycle instead of a heavy sedan. I sat in the front seat and forgot how to breathe.

The girls, squished in the back, never noticed how close we came to head-on, side, and rear-end collisions during the ride. They pressed up against the windows. I clutched my seat with white knuckles. From time to time they caught a glimpse of the Eiffel's unmistakable silhouette, and one of them, shrieking and pointing, would cry, "Oh my God, there it is!"

The driver dropped us at the base of the Eiffel Tower. I clambered out and stood on the street for a moment, silent, looking at the huge steel structure so tall it was hard to see the top of it. I resisted the urge to let my shaking legs fold so I could collapse to the ground. We each paid the cabdriver five euros, more than twice the metro fare, and I worked hard to ignore the metro sign ten feet away.

I was traveling with novices, I reminded myself. I would have to accept there'd be certain costs involved.

We walked toward the large, manicured park at the base of the tower. Of course, they posed and took dozens of pictures with the Eiffel Tower in the background. One at a time, two at a time, the three of them, the four of us, hamming it up for the camera.

"You can't come to Paris and not have a picture of you with the Eiffel Tower. Ze French, zey will arrest you." Lola kept saying everything in a French accent, and somehow even the dumbest things came out sounding funny.

To make up for Lola's missing camera, Katie and Madison spent almost half an hour taking pictures of Lola in front of the Eiffel before they were ready to move on. Or up, as it turned out.

"Of course we're going up," Lola said. "You can't come all the way here and not go to the top of the Eiffel Tower. Ze French, zey will arrest you!"

Madison giggled in excitement, and the three of them hurried to the ticket booth. I brought up the rear, feeling tired and out of place. Ahead of me, they linked arms and were doing chorus-line kicks.

"Come on, Arden," Katie called out. "Join us!"

Be cool, I thought. They were nice, they were keyed up over Paris. I liked them and chose to join them. The thought that my plane to Frankfurt was probably taking off now drifted through my mind, but I pushed it away.

It bothered me that I wasn't dressed more "French." That old urge to blend in kicked into gear. If I didn't speak and just smiled small coy smiles while looking haughty, I could be French, even with my curly blond-brown hair and hazel eyes. I needed to wear a skirt with no hose and high-heeled sandals. My hair would be off my face in a twist.

To fit in with the Texans, though, I needed to wear shorts, a tank top, and flip-flops. I'd wear sunglasses, chew gum, and carry a water bottle. I'd talk and laugh and point, and no one looking at the four of us would guess I'd met them less than twenty-four hours ago.

Instead, I was dressed for the plane ride and for landing in Germany. I was wearing jeans with blue tennis shoes (Americans wear white ones), and my hair was up but not tidy. I didn't fit with anyone.

But that was the problem, after all. I didn't fit in anywhere.

4.

The line to buy tickets snaked back and forth, and a sign above the ticket booth flashed the news in several languages that it would take two hours to get to the front. I winced at the prices. You could get off at different levels: the first level, the square that sat like low-riding jeans on the hips of the tower; the second level, just above it, or you could go all the way up to the square-headed top of the tower.

The stairs were free.

"Did you guys want to go to the first level?" I asked hopefully.

"No way," Lola said. "If we're going, we're going to the top, baby!" She high-fived Madison. Katie caught my look, and we exchanged smiles. She tilted her head a bit, as if to say, "How about it?"

I heard myself say, "I've never been to the top before, but I've heard it's amazing."

An hour and a half later, sweating and parched, we reached the ticket booth and paid eleven euros each.

In the elevator, people pressed in until there was hardly room to move. The many warnings to beware of pickpockets displayed throughout the waiting area flashed through my mind, but in the elevator there wasn't much I could do to protect my small travel pack, riding diagonally across my back. It was also remarkably stuffy and hot. The French didn't bother with AC in the elevator. The steel skeleton of the Eiffel flew by as we ascended its spindly leg.

I started feeling nauseous.

The elevator stopped; we got off, switched elevators, and continued to the top. Without opening my backpack, I touched the compartment where I kept my wallet and made sure it was still there.

I stepped out to the viewing deck, and a strong gust of wind blew my hair into my eyes. By the time I untangled myself, the rest of the girls had rushed out and were oohing at the view.

"Don't you feel like you could just fly away?" Madison said, her voice wistful, even a little sad.

Paris stretched out before me, out and out in all directions. I spotted the Arc de Triomphe off to the right, looking like a Monopoly playing piece. The Seine meandered through the city like a fat, lazy snake.

"I just love this," Lola said. "Look how amazing the streets look, and the buildings—God, this is awesome!" She bounded over to Madison, and the two of them did an impromptu tango. Katie snapped a couple of pictures, and a few people clapped when Madison dipped Lola.

I closed my eyes for a second and let the cool air whip all around me. The air felt clean up here, not like the tepid, smoggish air on the ground. Even with my cynicism and my stamp-filled passport, being here and seeing all of Paris below me reminded me that Paris was special and beautiful.

When I was little, I thought you could reach heaven if you climbed high enough. I even asked my dad why no one had built an elevator so people could go up to see heaven and not be scared of dying. I don't remember his answer.

Up here now, as I stood as high up in the air as I'd ever been, the thought flashed through my mind that I still wasn't high enough but that maybe my younger self was on to something. My problems seemed smaller at this height.

"Dad?" I whispered, closing my eyes. "Am I getting close?"

I held my breath, waiting to see if I felt anything, heard an echo of his voice, felt the touch of his hand on my face. Instead, I was jostled sideways by a large German man and snapped my eyes open to keep from falling.

"I can't believe I'm on the Eiffel Tower and I don't have anyone to kiss!" It was Lola, of course. I saw people exchange smiles, while some rolled their eyes.

Madison reached for her, like she was going in for a kiss, and Lola shrieked and ran away. I smiled but stepped back, separating myself from them.

Katie walked up to me, and we leaned our elbows on the railing and looked out, the breeze tangling our hair.

"Are you thinking about your mom?" she asked, seeing the melancholy look on my face. "It's hard to believe there's anything wrong with the world from up here," she said. Paris spread below our feet.

"I know," I said. "I feel the same."

It was true. I did feel peaceful, even with the interruptions. I savored the feeling. At eleven euros, it was a bargain.

"Is anyone else hungry?" Madison asked, joining us at the rail.

"I am," I said.

"Me too," Lola said.

"All right, then," Katie said. "Let's *vámonos*." She paused. "I don't know how to say that in French."

"*Allez-vous?*" Madison suggested. "*On y va?*"

"Are we going to vote on this?" Lola said. "Because if we're speaking French election–style, then, ladies, we might have a problem."

"I think *on y va* sounds right," I said. "And what's wrong with voting anyway?"

"There's nothing wrong with voting," Lola said. "I think voting is great. I do it early and often."

We waited another fifteen minutes for the elevator to come, and then my stomach dropped as we descended.

By the time we made it to the ground, it was past one.

"I have seriously bad news," I said when I saw how late it was. "If we don't get to a restaurant soon, we'll be stuck without any food until dinner, and dinner starts late here."

"What? Why?" Madison said in alarm.

"Everything closes at two. It's like siesta. We better hurry."

Katie pulled out her guidebook and flipped through the tabbed and annotated Paris restaurant section to figure out the closest place to eat.

"Jesus, Katie," Madison said, switching weight from foot to foot like a child waiting in line for the bathroom. "We don't have to eat only where the guidebook says; we just need to find a place."

"I found one," Katie said. "'Charming bistro with rustic setting . . . traditional family cuisine . . . excellent value.'"

"Great, but where is it?"

"Left," she said. "Rue Claire." Madison grabbed my hand, and I laughed out loud as we pulled ahead of Katie and Lola. We ran for blocks and Madison kept gasping for me to slow down, but when Lola and Katie tried to pass, she pulled on my arm to make me run faster. The streets were noticeably quiet and empty. After two wrong turns and walking right by the restaurant without noticing it, we eventually figured out where the place was, and even though the waiter wasn't happy to see us, he sat us at a dark "rustic" table in the back.

The menu, perhaps not surprisingly, was completely in French.

"Don't worry," Madison said when Lola groaned. "I took four years of French in high school, remember?"

"Are we going to be voting again?" Lola asked.

"Let's see here," Madison said, ignoring her. "I'm pretty sure that *laitue* is some kind of vegetable."

"That's helpful," Lola said. "All in favor say 'aye.'"

"*Dinde* is pork. I'm almost sure. No, wait, it's chicken. No, shit! I don't know." She threw the menu down in disgust.

Katie did a bit better, looking up words in the tiny glossary in the back of the guidebook, but most of the words weren't there.

"What kind of glossary doesn't have basic menu items? I'm definitely writing a letter to the editor," she said.

I didn't speak French either, so I ended up ordering a salad, which was easy to figure out since it's called *salade* in French. Even if there were something on it that I didn't like, it'd be easy to take it off. How could you go wrong with a salad?

Lola decided to do the same, but Madison wanted something "French." In halting French, accented so strongly with a Texas twang that even I cringed, Madison asked the waiter to recommend something.

He paused for a second, perhaps stunned into mild paralysis by her butchered pronunciation. But then she smiled, and before he could stop himself, I saw him smile back.

"*J'ai faim,*" she said in a Texas twang, rubbing her stomach. As if on cue, it rumbled and she giggled.

I could see him visibly melt before her blue eyes, large in her tiny heart-shaped face. He leaned over her to point to the prix fixe dish on the handwritten menu. She looked up at him from under his outstretched arm.

"*Mercy buckets,*" she said. At least that's what it sounded like to me.

The waiter inclined his head in welcome.

The girls all giggled. We were watching a master at work.

Katie decided to order the waiter's choice as well, which included an entrée, dessert, and coffee. Considering how much came with it, I thought it was a good deal. But it also cost a good deal more than ordering a single entrée.

"*Et une carafe* of *vin rouge.*" Madison pointed to the line on the menu that listed wines.

"Ah . . . Madison?" Katie said.

"We're in *France,*" she whispered back. "He *expects* us to order wine with lunch."

Katie looked over at Lola, but Lola just shrugged.

"The drinking age here is, like, ten, and the French drink red wine with everything," she said. "You can't be in Paris and not drink wine with your meal."

"Fine," Katie said. "When in Paris, right? But let's order a bottle of water too."

Lola, a vegetarian, changed her mind on the salad and ordered a different prix fixe entrée that the waiter assured her had no meat. At least that's what we thought he said. The no-meat "ayes" had it.

"How long have you known each other?" I asked when the waiter left.

"Madison and Lola know each other from high school," Katie said. "Right?"

"Middle school," Lola said.

"We met Katie the first week of college," Madison added. "At freshman orientation."

"That's great," I said. I tried to suppress the flashbacks of my college freshman orientation. The stupid get-to-know-you games, the instant cliques that I wasn't part of, the bewildering sense that everyone was having fun but me.

"What's it like to grow up a military brat?" Katie asked. "It must be so different, moving around all the time."

"Military brats have their own advantages," I said. "But unfortunately, lifelong childhood friendships isn't one of them." I meant to sound light and casual, but it didn't come out that way.

There was a short, awkward pause before Madison launched into the story of how she and Lola met.

"My dog, Lady, was insane about chasing things. You could throw her anything, and she would tear after it. We were at a park, and my brother throws this pinecone over the edge of a low stone fence, and the next thing we know, Lady's after it. She sails over the wall and disappears. So we run after her, and that's when we realize there was, literally, like a thirty-foot drop on the other side."

I don't know if it was stress or jet lag, but for some reason, I started to laugh. I tried not to, but the more I tried holding it back, the more it bubbled up.

"We thought she'd been killed," Madison said, looking at me oddly.

"We were having a picnic in this nice open field with a tall stone wall to lean against," Lola said. "Next thing we know, this dog lands on our picnic blanket, smashing the basket with all our food."

By now I was nearly crying, I was laughing so hard. Katie joined in with giggles, and Lola and Madison looked pleased with themselves.

"We're like, 'What was that? It's raining dogs!'"

"Lady was fine, in case you were wondering," Madison scolded us. "And she got a lot better about not jumping over fences. Lola and I have been friends ever since."

When the food finally came, the smell made my mouth fill with saliva. I felt deliciously weak from the laughter and the wine floating through my veins.

With a small flourish, the waiter placed each plate in front of us. Katie and Madison, as it turned out, had ordered a roasted chicken in a golden sauce, with herbed potatoes and buttery carrots that smelled and looked wonderful. They cooed with delight.

Lola received a huge white plate with a golden, crusty quiche bursting with spinach and cheese.

Feeling like a contestant in a game show, I turned to see my prize. But like many hopeful contestants, I'd picked the wrong door. My salad, though generous, consisted of mixed greens, some sort of dark, musty-smelling mushrooms in heavy oil, anchovies, boiled potatoes, green beans, and corn. I had expected something light and crisp and cool. The smell of moldy leather and a faint whiff of fish went a long way to cool hunger.

"This is freaking awesome!" Lola said.

She cut the quiche, which practically fell apart as she

breathed on it, and moaned with pleasure. "This is what all the books write about. This is Paris."

Madison and Katie dug into their meals with the vigor and gusto of cowboys who'd been working on the range all day without a break. There was hardly any talk at all as each girl concentrated on the masterpiece that was her first meal in Paris.

I looked at my salad. The anchovies looked back.

It galled me that I'd paid so much for so little. Holding my breath, I started eating the salad, avoiding the actual chunks of turdlike mushrooms and the fish but tasting them in the oil that glistened on every forkful.

Now that the worst of the girls' hunger had been sated, Lola insisted that Katie and Madison taste her quiche, and Madison fed Lola some potatoes and carrots. They looked over at me.

"You want to try?"

"Sure."

Lola placed a bite's worth on my bread plate, carefully avoiding the fish I'd exiled there. Katie put a piece of chicken and some carrots next to it. I tasted each, and they were so good I was amazed they agreed to share even the little they had with me. The chicken tasted almost creamy. The quiche was sweet and salty, with some sort of tangy cheese that I'd never tasted before but fell in love with in an instant.

"I think I've lost voting privileges," I said. "I managed to order the only bad meal in Paris. But if you want to try some, you're welcome to it."

They looked at each other.

"With an endorsement like that, who could resist?" Lola said.

"Anchovies are good for you," I pitched. "They're full of omega-three fatty acids. Anyone interested?"

"You're so good, eating a salad," Katie said, ducking the question. "No wonder you're so skinny. I think I've already gained three pounds." It was a sweet thing to say, but Katie and I were about the same size. In fact, we looked a bit alike with the same tawny coloring, except that her light brown hair was tidy and straight while mine was in higgledy-piggledy curls. Besides, we both knew that even if she did gain weight, that chicken was worth every pound.

Lola declined on account of the fish, and Katie insisted she was full, but in the end, adventurous Madison decided that since I had ordered the salad in Paris, how bad could it be? She tasted it, made a noncommittal *mm* sound, and refreshed her glass of water.

"You're definitely on voting probation," she said, which made Lola laugh.

"Okay, I've got to try it," Katie said, working up the nerve. She took a taste and made a face.

"Oh, Arden," she said. "What were you thinking? You should have sent it back. It's awful!"

"Thanks," I said. "That makes me feel better. No, really. It does."

The prix fixe meal they ordered came with dessert, so I watched them enjoy another course, a light, meringue-topped lemon tart. Katie kindly shared half of it with me. At least it got the taste of fish out of my mouth.

I tried to block out the sound of the ticking clock in my head and the rumbling in my stomach. It was getting late, and I didn't have a place booked for the night.

"It's three o'clock," Katie announced, glancing at her watch. "Are we cool to just split the bill four ways?"

I bit my tongue in protest. My salad cost six euros. Their

prix fixe meals were twelve euros each. But we were in a hurry, and it seemed petty to fight over a few dollars.

"Sure," I said, and everyone else nodded.

"Okay girls," Madison said, bill in hand. "The total's fifty-one euros, plus we need the tip."

"Actually," I said, "in Europe you don't tip that much. . . ." Usually you rounded up to the nearest whole number, since waiters received a normal salary and didn't live from tips.

"No way," she said flatly. "I was a waitress; there's nothing worse than when someone stiffs you. I always leave a big tip." There was no budging her. I ended up paying fifteen euros for a nasty salad, water, and a glass of wine. With the exchange rate what it was, this was probably the most expensive lunch I'd ever had.

We left the restaurant, and Katie flagged another cab to take us back to the train station. We rode in silence, the three of them digesting their wonderful meals and me adding up numbers trying to figure out how much I'd already spent in the hours since I'd arrived.

We got our bags and took *another* cab to the hostel. We arrived in front of a charming little building, and I perked up thinking that I'd never have found it without them. For twenty bucks a night, I could afford to splurge, even on bad food.

"You guys go first," I said at the check-in counter. "It'll probably take longer for me since I don't have a reservation yet."

"This place used to be a convent," Katie told me while they waited for the receptionist to get their room key. "There're four beds in each room instead of the huge barracks-style beds in most hostels. Hopefully, they'll just give you the fourth bed in our room. I mean, what are the chances that it's already filled?"

Finally they had their key and I was next.

"We're going to drop our stuff," Katie said.

"I'll wait for you down here," I said, waving her off. "In case we don't get assigned to the same room."

"See you in a bit!"

"Hi," I said, stepping up to the counter.

"*Bonjour,*" said the crisp-looking woman. Her hair was up in a twist, and she had small pearl earrings in her tiny earlobes. She looked elegant and casual, and I thought that it was true, there was something special about Parisian women. "What is your name?" she asked coolly.

"Arden Vogel." She started typing. "But wait—" I said. "I don't have a reservation. I wanted to make one."

"Very good. For which nights?"

"For tonight. I'm not sure how many nights, maybe three. It depends on—"

"I'm sorry," she cut me off. "We are full through the end of the week. Would you care to make a reservation for next week?"

"What?"

"We are full."

"I just need one bed."

"We have nothing. I am sorry. The last bed was taken two hours ago. I cannot help you." Her tone couldn't have been less interested or sympathetic.

"Oh. Okay." I tried to think past the crushing weight of disappointment. "Um, do you have a recommendation for some other place I could try?"

"No."

"Oh." I was silent for a moment. "Okay. Thanks."

She nodded as if getting thanked for being utterly unhelpful was only her due. I changed my mind about her elegance and sophistication.

Luckily, there was a pay phone in the lobby. A lobby, I

noted sourly, with comfortable-looking couches and large windows and healthy plants.

I took a deep breath and tried to keep the situation in perspective. I told that sinking feeling in my stomach to relax. I spotted a European guidebook in English amidst the abandoned paperbacks on the little bookshelf in the lobby; it had recommendations; I wasn't helpless. Maybe I'd find something even better on my own, a terrific *pension* with a calico cat and a rooftop garden. I opened the guidebook and started calling the various hostels it listed.

Ten minutes later, I was fighting tears. All the hostels in Paris were full. *All of them.* One of the men I spoke to actually laughed when I asked for a bed for tonight. The combination of jet lag and no sleep in twenty hours brutally caught up with me.

Reluctantly, I started calling the one- and two-star hotels listed. At first I called only the places that the book called "charming," "quaint," or "an excellent value." None of them had a single room.

Why did I get off in Paris? Why didn't I make the call to the hostel right away? They had phone directories in Paris. I hadn't even tried. And I *knew* this was going to happen. It would have taken five minutes to call and reserve my bed. I wanted to scream.

Instead, I kept dialing.

When one of the places I tried actually said yes, he had a room, I felt such a rush of relief that my knees went a little weak. For a moment, I'd had visions of sleeping on a park bench.

"I will hold it for you for one hour," he said. "You must come pay for it in one hour or I give it away."

"I'll be there. I promise. Don't give it away."

I hung up just in time to see Katie, Madison, and Lola traipse down the stairs, laughing.

"Arden, wait until you see the rooms. They are so amazing! They have these high ceilings with actual frescoes on them and the beds are wrought-iron—"

"They're out of room here," I said, trying not to sound as bitter as I felt. "So I found another place and I have to go right away because they'll only hold the room for an hour."

"Oh no." Katie seemed distressed. "That sucks."

I shrugged.

"Dude, can you call your dad?" Lola asked. "I mean, he might help out. Since it's going to cost so much more than you expected?" I'd told Katie my dad had died two and a half years ago. She must not have told the others. I saw her glare at Lola.

"No. I'm all right. My dad's not around anymore." I swallowed and tried to smile. "This is my adventure and I'll stick it out."

"Listen, we have tickets to the Moulin Rouge tonight," Madison said, turning away from browsing a French fashion magazine lying on an end table and joining the conversation. "You have to come and meet us there. I'm sure you could buy a ticket at the door."

"Yeah, sure," I said.

"It's at eight. We'll wait for you outside, okay?"

"Yeah, totally," I said. I even sort of meant it. What else would I do on my first night in Paris, sit alone in a hotel room?

"Awesome. Okay, see you tonight."

"Take a cab, okay?" Katie said. "You shouldn't take the metro with your luggage by yourself."

"Don't worry about it."

Katie hugged me and I hugged her back. "See you tonight."

Since I was scared to get lost and miss my one-hour window, I gritted my teeth and paid for a taxi to take me straight there.

I took the guidebook with me.

The cab stopped in front of a dingy door with trash on the sidewalk. I hoped the driver had stopped because there was something in the road, or someone crossing the street.

He grunted something.

"What?"

"Hôtel Jardin," he grunted again, this time pointing out the window.

This was my hotel? I took a deep breath. *Okay.*

The front door was locked, and I pressed the call button to be buzzed in. I hoped to be pleasantly surprised once inside, but no. It was gloomy and dark, and from what I could see, the couch sagged in the middle and tilted to the side. A dim bulb illuminated the front desk.

"Hi," I said, reluctantly walking over. "We spoke on the phone? I'm here for the room."

Without looking away from the show on the tiny television mounted on the wall, the man, cigarette dangling from his lips, pushed over a small paper.

"Fill out. Cash only. No refund."

I wrote in my name, my address, my passport number, my reason for visiting. Under how many nights staying, I put one. It cost fifty-five euros for the night. Almost seventy bucks. The man took my money and slid it straight into his pocket.

Again, without looking away from the television, he reached over and grabbed a key with an oversized plastic number dangling from it and handed it to me.

"Fifth floor," he rasped, ashes from his cigarette sprinkling down. "Toilet down the hall."

I began trudging up the dark, narrow staircase, smoldering at the thought that fifty-five euros a night hadn't even gotten me my own bathroom.

The narrow door opened and I stood there, looking at the room in despair. The lobby was elegant and cheery compared to my room. There were huge dark stains on the buckled carpet. The bed, a tiny box, had visible lumps and a deep depression in the center as if a body had lain on it for years. There was a small sink, stained yellow, and a steady drip-drip from the faucet. The room smelled too. Besides the mold and dust, the unmistakable scent of urine hung over the sink, silent testimony to the many guests who didn't feel like leaving the room to use the bathroom.

You'd think after nearly three years I'd know how futile it was to wish for things to magically become undone, for time to go back, for me to disappear. You'd think I'd know there was no point blaming anyone but myself for the things that went wrong. But I did. I blamed all of them for asking me to join them in the first place; who does that? I blamed Katie for talking me out of calling the hostel right away.

I joined them because I thought they needed me, I thought they wouldn't be able to handle traveling through Europe; but I was beginning to see that I was the one who needed help. I was the one who made the most novice mistake of waiting too late to book a room. It was the first thing you did, not the last, especially during the heavily traveled summer season.

Through this past year at college, I'd mostly kept to myself. I hadn't lived in the United States for two years, and even then, it was always on an army post. I'd felt out of place in Nashville, with its music scene and its southern ways. Coming to Europe, I thought, would feel like coming home.

But it didn't.

5.

I was going into eleventh grade when we moved to Germany. Even though it meant breaking up my high school years, I was all for the move.

We'd never spent much time in Germany before, and one of the first things we noticed was that Germans took driving very seriously. Their cars were perfectly maintained and gleaming clean. I never saw a clunker with a smoky tailpipe on the road unless it had American plates. The left lane was used *only* for passing. Turn signals *always* blinked before a turn. German cars came with two horn settings—a muted one to use inside town and a louder one to blast through the rushing wind of the speed-limitless autobahn. But even so, I hardly ever heard a bleep or a peep from a German car. They didn't need it. Everyone followed the rules of the road. Germans always follow the rules.

Most of the German driving laws were the same as those in the States. They drove on the right side of the road, passed on the left. Stop signs were red and looked like the ones in the

States. Speed limits, though in kilometers, were clearly marked and obvious.

In fact, there was only one truly different rule: cars coming from the right at an intersection had the right of way. Sometimes if the straight road was major enough, like a city thoroughfare, then there was a yellow and white diamond posted to indicate that you didn't need to brake for cars coming from right-handed streets. Otherwise, without any stop signs or yield signs, while driving straight, even on major town roads, you were supposed to slow down and check streets on the right for oncoming traffic.

This was counterintuitive to most Americans. Driving down a straight road, they found it hard to remember that cars coming from the right perpendicular had the right of way, especially when many of the roads were exempted from this rule. The roads where the rule held firm were usually quiet and without much traffic, so the likelihood of running through the intersection at the exact moment a German driver came hurtling through, confident of their safe passage, was slim.

But not impossible.

The irony was that my dad loved driving in Germany. Loved how smoothly the rules of the road worked when everyone followed them.

"German drivers are so much better than Americans," he said on more than one occasion, usually as we cruised at ninety miles an hour. He cringed when some SUV or minivan with American plates held up a German-plated Mercedes. It would cruise obliviously in the left lane while the German pulled within inches of its bumper and repeatedly flicked his headlights at them to no avail.

"I like it," he said when my mom teased him. "Everybody knows what the rules are and they follow them. Driving is such a pleasure here. And I think it's great that no one crosses an empty street if the pedestrian light is red."

My mom and I groaned. Germans would wait until the light turned green before they crossed the road. One even wagged a finger at me when I crossed an empty street while the light was still red.

We laughed that my dad's German blood was showing. Vogel was a German name, though it was a great-great-grandparent who'd last lived in Germany.

"Did you know that some Germans have 'driving shoes'?" Dad told us with glee. "I saw a man getting out of his car and changing out of his special shoes that he wore only inside the car."

"How do you know that?" I asked. "You're making it up."

"I asked. He told me."

Even though my mom was the one in the military, my dad was the one who liked to follow the rules. Maybe it came from the fact that he dealt with mathematical equations during the day. Maybe if you lived surrounded by a world of precision, where failure to follow rules always meant professional failure, it colored your view of the world.

My mom belonged to the school of "don't ask the question if you think you won't like the answer." She believed in thinking for yourself. Not that my dad didn't. It's just that his way of thinking and my mom's didn't seem to come from the same source.

Usually I was more like my dad than my mom. I liked turning in my homework on time. I didn't skip school. I liked dressing neatly and hated it if in the morning rush I put on socks that didn't match. I'd go through the whole school day feeling uncomfortable and restless.

And here I was in Paris, not following the rules.

I wasn't sure what I'd expected to get out of joining Katie and her friends in Paris, but whatever it was, I hadn't found it. I was alone. My dad was gone; my mom was unreachable.

After my dad died and it was the two of us, there was hardly a day my mom and I were apart. She hated living alone in the apartment once I left for college. I think she was slightly relieved when the deployment came up. We talked on the phone almost every day until she deployed, and now my contact with her had been reduced to reading pixels on a screen. If something happened to her, I believed I might disintegrate. There would be nothing left to keep me together.

6.

After sitting on the lumpy bed in my crappy Parisian hotel for ten minutes, my head in my hands, I suddenly remembered that I was supposed to e-mail my mom as soon as I landed in Germany.

As always when I thought about my mom, I felt guilty for thinking my life was hard.

My mom had a fifteen-minute "commute" from her trailer to the hospital, passing rows of trailers like rows of grinning teeth, like Chiclets before they get packaged in their blister packs. It was hot and dusty, and on days when the post was on high alert, she walked in full "battle rattle": a Kevlar flak jacket, helmet, and her personal weapon, a nine millimeter, in a holster on her hip.

When she first arrived, she was overwhelmed by the jet lag, the heat, the sickening knowledge she was in Kuwait, headed for Iraq.

Her body armor was unfamiliar and she wasn't used to wearing a weapon. The cheap holster had gotten tangled over her body armor. Without even asking, a squared-away-looking warrant officer untangled her gear. They started chatting. He was on his second tour.

"I don't envy you," he said, seeing her branch insignia.

As she looked at his uniform, she realized he was a helicopter pilot.

"Ditto," she said.

It's the baby nurses my heart goes out to, my mom wrote in one of her later e-mails. *These girls graduated nursing school a few months ago, and they're seeing every awful thing that can happen to a body in Iraq, and that's saying a lot. Their pale desert combat boots are already black with blood.*

What about your *boots,* I wanted to ask. *Aren't they soaked with blood as well?*

What was a crappy hotel room or selling a vacation home compared to life in the barracks, working twelve-hour shifts? She had to deal with dying Iraqi babies and soldiers with missing limbs and burned-off faces. I had to deal with the fact that my vacation wasn't as fabulous as I'd hoped.

I headed out into the warm Paris evening, trying to push away thoughts of the depressing hotel, my awful room, and to keep things in perspective. It was just one night. It was just a hotel. It didn't mean I was a failure.

I found an Internet café and paid for an hour. The first thing I did was check my Hotmail account. I had a message from Peter Meyer, three ads for penile enlargements, one for getting a PhD online within a year, and two for refinancing my home. I scanned past all of them, looking for a message from my mom.

Every time I logged on, my heart beat faster and my palms grew sweaty. I had to have a message from her. People in school talked about waiting for a guy to call them back, checking their cells religiously. I didn't check my e-mail to know if my mom liked me; I checked to know she was alive.

It was there and I clicked it open.

Darling—hope the flight went well. Who did you decide to stay with on post?

Before I'd left, I hadn't decided which of our military friends to stay with in Heidelberg.

Things here are fine. We finally had a few quiet days. It was such a relief to actually sleep for eight hours. I'd almost forgotten how nice that is.

There's talk that they're going to launch fireworks for the Fourth of July. I told the commander what a bad idea that was. I don't think people with post-traumatic stress need more explosions, even if they're pretty ones. The fact that this is coming from the MWR people is just too ironic. This won't help Morale, Welfare, or provide much Recreation. As you can imagine, I'm on a mission to eradicate patriotic fever. I am a nurse, after all. I'm naturally inclined against fevers.

Hey, Mom, I wrote her back. *You'll never guess where I am . . . Paris!* I didn't tell her about my hotel. She'd worry that it wasn't safe, and she'd be right. The fact that I was in Paris instead of Heidelberg would throw her off enough. *I met three college girls from the University of Texas and they talked me into getting off at my layover and hanging out with them in the City of Light.*

Since Sardinia is about as close to Paris as it is to Heidelberg, I figured why not? There's no great reason for me to go to Heidelberg, and it's been so long since I'd visited Paris. Not since you, Dad, and I went when I was ten.

I hope you're not upset, I wrote. *And listen, I think there's a vaccine for patriotic fever.*

Stay safe. I love you a lot and I'll write more tomorrow.

I always wrote that, always promised something for the next

day. I didn't want her to think that I thought something might happen to her. She knew that I worried, of course, but this way we could both pretend things were normal.

After I sent my mom her e-mail, I read Peter's.

Peter and I had first met each other at Fort Riley in Kansas when I was in fourth grade, he was in fifth, and we lived on the same street. I don't remember being close friends, but we did walk to school together for a whole year. The only vivid memory I have of that time was the day there was a sudden tornado warning.

Heavy rainstorms were expected later in the day, but sirens blasted during our walk to school. They were so loud and unexpected that I stopped in the middle of the sidewalk and clapped my hands over my ears, looking around for a police car or ambulance. I had never lived in a tornado area, and I had no idea there were sirens to warn that a tornado was coming. People stopped what they were doing, and after scanning the sky, they raced to shelters. The leaden clouds and the moist, heavy air suddenly seemed ominous.

"What's going on?" I shouted.

Peter, who had lived in Kansas for two years and knew what a tornado siren meant, grabbed my hand, and we ran to the nearest building. He led the way to the staircase, never letting go of my hand, and we sprinted to the basement. We huddled in the corner with other people from the building until the sirens stopped. When we climbed back up the stairs, everything looked the same. The tornado hadn't touched down inside the fort, but I felt jittery and nervous for the rest of the day. At school we heard that several houses in the town outside the post were completely destroyed, nothing left but the concrete stairs at the front.

At the end of the year, Peter moved, and I didn't see him again or think about him until my junior year in Heidelberg.

Even in elementary school Peter swam in competitive leagues. That was probably part of the reason we weren't closer friends. He was hardly ever around. Nearly every weekend we would see a loaded station wagon heading out to swim practice, swim meets, or extra lessons with the coach at the pool.

After we moved to Heidelberg, it didn't take long for me to hear all about our killer swim team.

"That's him, that's the captain of the swim team," Amber hissed in my ear during lunch. I knew Amber from eighth grade, when we were both at Fort Sam Houston in Texas.

We were sitting in the cafeteria when a guy with the perfect swimmer's body walked by. He was probably six-three, with long legs, large hands, and broad shoulders.

"He holds four school records," she whispered. I hardly recognized him except that when he smiled, it was the same smile from fifth grade.

"Is his name Peter?" I asked, watching as he flirted with a preppy girl.

"You know him?" Amber asked. "Oh my God, that is so cool!"

"I think we were in elementary school together." I stood up before I'd realized it.

"You're not going over there. Sit down!" She grabbed my arm and yanked. "I don't think you understand. He's the coolest guy in school. You might be a junior, but you're not a jock. Peter, on the other hand"—she ticked off on her fingers—"is a senior, swim team captain, and as you can see, ridiculously hot. He won't give you the time of day."

"I'm just going to say hi."

Amber watched as I strolled over to him and introduced myself.

"Arden." He smiled in happy surprise. "It's been years."

"I know. Seen any tornadoes lately?"

He chuckled at my lame joke, and the girl he was talking to shot me a nasty look.

"Listen, Peter," she said, placing a small, manicured hand on his biceps. "Like I was saying, there's a wicked party this weekend. Are you coming?"

"I didn't mean to interrupt," I said, interrupting her again. "I'll see you around, Peter."

"See you later." He waved and then turned his attention back to the girl. I returned to my seat next to Amber.

"He wasn't," I said, whispering quietly and feeling my heart beat too fast, "nearly that hot in elementary school."

Amber snorted, and I pretended to fan myself with a napkin.

After that, I made it my job to find out more about Peter. He spent every morning and afternoon at the pool. The butterfly was his best event, but he was strong in freestyle as well. Every time I passed him in the hallways, he smelled vaguely of chlorine.

He was always nice to me, but he was surrounded by girls, and he was devoted to swimming. There wasn't much I could do to compete with that.

This distant friendliness went on for a few months, and then my dad died.

After the accident, I couldn't focus; nothing seemed very important. I couldn't remember why I was shy with Peter; I couldn't think of why I got so nervous during exams. Amber couldn't make me laugh anymore, and the whole caste system of high school was as foreign and meaningless to me as insect hierarchy. Nothing seemed significant enough to make my heart race or my stomach gurgle in excitement.

In the days after the funeral, some of the students came up to me to let me know they were sorry, one at a time or in groups of two and three, all of us awkward during the stilted, almost formal exchange. Some of them wouldn't look at me, as if I carried some contagious grief disease. When I found a card from Peter in my locker, I didn't get excited; I didn't grab Amber, rush to the bathroom, and read it together with her, giggling, which was exactly what I'd have done a month earlier. Then again, a month earlier, there wouldn't have been a condolence card in my locker.

I slipped the card unopened into my back pocket to read later. I wasn't sure what Peter's card would say: a scrawled signature under the preprinted sympathy verse? I couldn't work up a sufficient degree of interest. When I remembered it a couple of days later, I dug through the laundry hamper and pulled it out of my jeans pocket, slightly wrinkled and worse for the wear. His handwriting was neat and clear.

I'm so sorry for your loss, he wrote. *I remember I had this funny conversation with your dad when we lived in Fort Riley. I had to wear a tie to some stupid event and I had untied the one my mom had left me. I knew I would get into so much trouble if I arrived there with no tie, and your dad was outside and he saw me. He helped me tie the one I had, and while I grumbled that ties were totally stupid, he said, "Well, if the ceremony gets too awful, you can always turn it into a lasso and escape. That or hang yourself, whichever puts you out of your misery first."*

Since I knew my dad's idea of a perfect tie was either a bolo tie or no tie, I could just imagine how sincere his lesson was.

It made me smile.

It's a fucked-up world we live in. Your dad was a good man. I'm really sorry for your loss. Your friend, Peter.

I touched the signed name lightly.

I kept Peter's note in my desk drawer for a while, touching it whenever I felt particularly blue. Part of the heartache of losing my dad was that no one in Germany had known him. We'd only lived there a few months when he died, and while people were shocked, no one grieved. Not like we did. Peter's card helped remind me that my dad had made a difference in people's lives, even if I didn't see much evidence of that in Heidelberg.

I ran into Peter a few days later, and I stopped him with a hand on his arm.

"I read your card," I said quietly. He bent his head to hear. "I didn't know you knew my dad. It was a nice card. So, thanks."

I started walking past when his hand on my arm stopped me.

"Arden," he said.

I looked up.

"Are you going to be okay?"

"Yeah," I said. What could I say?

"Good," he said. "That's good."

A week later, he came by as I was eating lunch, folding his long body into the plastic cafeteria chair. I could feel all the girls watching.

"So a bunch of us are catching a movie on Friday; do you want to come?"

The offer caught me by surprise.

"Uh, thanks," I said. "But I don't really feel like hanging out with a bunch of people yet."

"Actually," he said, looking a little uncomfortable, "I guess I didn't really mean a bunch of people. I was thinking maybe it would just be you and me."

For a second, for one wonderful moment, I felt my heart rate kick up. Peter was asking me out on a date. I liked him so much and I could feel all the girls watching us, dying to know what we were talking about.

I would have loved to go to a movie with him, spending two hours in the dark sitting right next to him, sharing popcorn, maybe going bowling afterward.

But I couldn't say yes. My heartbeat slowed back down to its normal sedate rate. Before my dad died, Peter and I hadn't even talked, and now, a few weeks after his death, Peter was asking me out on a date. I didn't want something good to come out of my dad's death.

And what if Peter was asking me out because he felt sorry for me?

Without looking up from my sandwich, I shook my head.

"I don't think that would be a good idea," I said.

"Oh."

"Yeah, I think . . . well, I just think—" I tried to think of something that would soften the rejection.

"It's okay, Arden," he said. "Don't feel like you have to give me a reason."

"It wouldn't be right," I said.

"I didn't mean it that way," he said quickly.

"No, it was sweet," I said, forcing myself to look up from my mangled sandwich. "It's just that, you know . . ." I shrugged.

"Sure, no problem."

I knew I shouldn't watch him walk away, but I did.

He never asked me out again, but an odd sort of friendship remained, and if we passed each other, we'd stop in the hallway to chat.

"What's the swim team going to do without you when you graduate?" I asked him after spring break. It was hard to imagine this school without him.

"I don't know. Disband, I guess."

I snorted.

"I don't want to be spreading rumors, but word is Coach Tillman is plotting with Ms. Feyder to flunk you in English."

"Thanks for the tip, Sherlock," he said, punching me lightly on the shoulder. "I'll have to watch my dangling participles."

I couldn't stop myself from sneaking a peek over my shoulder, watching him amble away, looking so relaxed in his body the way only athletes seem to be.

A week later, he was recruited to Stanford on a swimming scholarship. When he graduated, I thought it would be the last time I'd see or hear from him. It's the only excuse I have for what happened between us on graduation night.

But a few weeks after he started college, I got an e-mail from him. It was very casual and friendly, asking about people at school, about the situation in Germany. He didn't mention the graduation party or our kiss, that one ridiculous, embarrassing, lovely kiss. Before I knew it, we were e-mailing each other a couple times a week. It was like having a delicious secret. I didn't tell anyone about our correspondence. It was a thrill, a tame one, a bit of fun in a dark year.

When I started Vanderbilt and felt so out of place, I appreciated his e-mails even more. Somehow he had become one of my best friends. It was a strange world in which I hadn't seen or spoken to my "best friend" in close to two years, and one where he became my best friend only once we lived two thousand miles away from each other.

When my mom told me about her deployment, he was the first person I wrote to, and his answering e-mail was the most helpful. His dad had recently returned from a year there, and he wrote how worried he'd been and how helpless he felt.

So now, after reading his e-mail about how he saw George Clooney at a café near campus, I e-mailed back about my impulsive stop in Paris. I didn't need to sugarcoat it like I did for my mom. It wasn't like Peter would lose sleep worrying about me.

Hey, P.—I think I might be going crazy. I got off at the layover in Paris. I'm here now, staying at this nasty hotel, and I'm wondering what the heck I'm even doing here. Please tell me this is normal. I met these Texas girls on the flight over and I started talking to one of them. I told her all about my mom, all the shit that's going on in Iraq and the horrible injuries she's dealing with, which you know I NEVER talk about, and then the next thing I know, she invited me to join them in Paris and I said yes. Except that to make a long story short, I didn't get a bed in their "fabulous" hostel, I didn't eat much lunch, and I'm already $200 poorer than I was this morning. What do you think, time to call a shrink, right? Au revoir, A.

After I finished with Hotmail, I tooled around the Web, checking up on my favorite sites, catching up on gossip and news.

I could almost forget I was in Paris. I could be anywhere—home, my dorm, safe and sound.

After my hour was up, I left the café. It was only six-thirty. Much too soon to go back to my room but too late to go to any museums or visit churches.

With nothing better to do, I decided to go to the Moulin Rouge Theatre and see if I could get a cheap student-rate ticket. The metro map was straightforward with color-coded lines and clearly marked stops. There was a comfortable number of travelers on the platforms waiting for trains. Two were clearly a couple, talking quickly and quietly, heads bent toward each other. There was a tired-looking woman with several grocery bags by her feet. I tried to see what was in them, but other than a head of lettuce and a bottle of mineral water, I couldn't make out much. A small gypsy urchin with a grubby round face and colorful clothes leaned against the wall.

The train arrived with a loud rumble and screech and we all stepped on board except the gypsy child.

I hadn't changed my clothes. As I disembarked from the metro station and walked to the theater, I regretted that. I shook my hair loose of its clip and retwisted it. I hoped it'd be enough.

I hurried through the darkening streets. The sun sank late during a Parisian June, but the tall buildings and narrow lanes created an artificially early twilight. I stumbled out of a dark alley into a bright, tree-lined boulevard and was struck again by Paris's odd tendency of having beautiful tree-lined streets with anachronistic cars parked bumper to bumper along the sidewalk. Old, ornate buildings managed to look both unoccupied and mysterious. Occasionally a light turning on or a curtain drawn proved that there was someone up there. But whether the apartment was full of heavily carved furniture, oil paintings, and a gourmet kitchen with a maid or water stains, rotting floorboards, and moldy mattresses was impossible for me to tell. The line between decay and opulence seemed thin here.

"*Bonjour,*" I said to the ticket lady in my best French accent. She was only a bit older than me, with dusky skin and chin-length coal black hair.

"*Bonsoir,*" she answered, slightly chiding.

"I'd like one ticket," I said, switching to English. "Student rate if you have it."

"One hundred and twenty-five euros," she said.

I gaped at her like a fish, stuttered for a moment, and then just to make sure I understood her right, I repeated slowly, "One hundred euros? Even for a student?"

Thinking that I might be confused, the woman wrote the figure on a piece of paper, leaving me no doubt.

I turned and left without saying another word. What was there to say?

I stomped my way back through the cobbled lanes of Montmartre, walking past cafés spilling into the narrow lanes full of people drinking and shouting and ordering another course, trying each other's entrées, and generally enjoying life to the fullest. Street artists sold tiny watercolor paintings, while a small crowd gathered around a group of street performers playing a lively polka.

The house in Sardinia beckoned to me like a warm light in the distance. I could go there. I could get on a train tomorrow to Bologna and catch a short flight to Sardinia from there. The sun would be hot. The food would be wonderful. I'd know my way around and I'd feel safe. I'd feel at home. Except that we were selling the house. That changed everything.

The first visit to Sardinia that I remember was when I was five and I made a friend. His name was Paolo and he was six. He found me crying by the shore. I had been following the lines the waves made in the sand, and when I looked up, I realized I couldn't find my parents.

How would we ever find each other again? The sea of blankets all looked the same.

"Mom!" I shouted, but only strangers turned to look. "Mom! Dad! Where are you?"

Strangers stopped.

"*Ragazza, cosa hai?*"

"Carina, perchè piangi?"

There was a circle of Italians crowded around me. The babble of Italian directed at me made me cry harder.

Everyone was so large and dark, and they spoke their gibberish quickly, their hands moving. By the time Paolo arrived, I was sobbing so hard I couldn't speak. He wove his way to the center to see what the commotion was and, being closer to my age, understood the situation without needing any words.

He took my hand, said something to the adults, and led me away. I held on tightly to his small brown hand and followed. I didn't understand what he was saying, but he was my size and he knew where he was going. Plus, I caught the word *mamma*. That was good enough for me.

He brought me to his parents' blanket. The next thing I knew, I was enveloped in a warm, sweaty hug from a woman with a large bosom that smelled of suntan oil. She stroked my hair, called me *"bella"*; and everything was all right.

She sat me down, opened the hamper, and pulled out dish after dish.

I wiped away my tears, blew my nose with the offered tissue, and settled in with my new family, instantly adopted.

My parents found me sitting in a stranger's lap eating a mozzarella and tomato sandwich.

After a joyous and tearful reunion, my parents joined Paolo's parents and we spent the afternoon together. Paolo and I played and splashed in the water while the adults sunned themselves and talked as best they could considering my parents' broken Italian. By the end of the afternoon, we'd been invited to join them for dinner.

We arrived at their cottage at nine o'clock, a reasonable dinnertime in Sardinia. My mother brought flowers, and we were ushered in, through the house and out to the porch that overlooked a small garden. Their house was closer to the beach, not on the mountain like ours.

We sat down with about ten other people. I never knew if they were relatives or friends or foundlings like us. It didn't matter. Everyone was cheerful and happy. There was the smell of food in the air, a promise of good things to come; and everyone was on vacation.

We had pizza with artichokes and mushrooms, layered salad with fresh mozzarella and garden-ripe tomatoes, stuffed red and yellow bell peppers, and fried eggplants. We had roasted chicken that fell off the bone, pasta with a lemony sauce, peas with mint, and marinated mushrooms. I guess I don't actually remember all of it, but I remember it through my parents' memories. Years later, they still talked about it as one of the best meals they'd ever had.

My mom made the mistake of trying to pass on one of the dishes. The looks of anguish and immediate pleas to try a little quickly convinced her that she must persevere and continue to eat or cause an international incident.

We ate one wonderful dish after another, each cooked to perfection, each so delicious we wondered what could possibly come next to top it. We ate until our stomachs hurt, but there were still more dishes to try.

Paolo sat next to me. By the end of the night, he spoke English and I spoke Italian. I don't remember not understanding him. He'd tell me what food came next and which were his favorites. When the adults lingered over a course, we'd get up and run to his room, where he would show me his toys. When the next course arrived, they shouted for us to return and we'd race back to our seats.

Dinner lasted over two hours. When it was through, the adults still sat at the table, too heavy and satiated to move. They lingered over their espresso and *mirto*, not wanting to leave. Paolo and I played in his room until we were tired. We lay down on his narrow bed, side by side like two young sardines, and fell asleep holding hands.

I woke up when my father laid me down in the backseat of the car.

"I didn't say goodbye," I said.

"Shhh, go to sleep," he said. "You'll see him tomorrow."

I played with Paolo every day for ten days. When our vacation was over and we had to leave, we hugged each other tightly. He and his mother bought me a bracelet, and I bought him a flashlight. I don't remember why anymore. But he was very happy with it, and I wore my bracelet every day until the cord wore away and I lost it.

I saw him again the next visit, when I was seven, and the visit after that, when I was nine. We were perfect playmates. Too young to worry about the fact that he was a boy and I was a girl. It didn't matter. We'd run and play in the sand and the waves. We'd climb the tall rock formations and spy on teenagers making out. We ate chocolate chip cookies and potato chips with my parents, then ran to his mom for focaccia with onions and rosemary.

When we came back two years later, he wasn't there. I made my parents drive past his cottage, but a different family was staying there. They were renting the cottage for the month; they didn't know anything about a boy named Paolo.

We had promised to meet again when we parted, swore we'd see each other next time.

At age eleven, with four army moves under my belt, I knew

that promises like that didn't keep. Still, even though I knew I shouldn't have expected him, I had.

It's possible that Paolo never returned to Sardinia or that he returned in years I wasn't there or even the same year but different weeks. They could have bought a bigger, better cottage. It's also possible that we'd both changed so much, we might have walked past each other on a crowded beach and never known it.

It's a lesson I had failed to learn again. Nothing lasted; people disappeared from your life as quickly and mysteriously as they appeared in the first place. To expect otherwise was to invite heartache.

I was busy with my memories, hardly noticing that I'd meandered back near the theater, when I heard my name called.

"Arden! Here! Over here!!"

There they were, dressed in jeans and sexy, shimmery tops. They looked like a picture you'd see in a brochure for a study-abroad program.

"Hey, you guys," I said, marshaling my happy face. I'd perfected it over the past few years. "You look great."

"Did you get a ticket?" Katie asked.

"No, they're too expensive."

"We bought ours online a couple of weeks ago," Madison rushed to explain. "Katie found this great site. We have tickets to tour Versailles tomorrow from there too."

"Oh." Of course they did. Why did I think they needed me?

"Are you going to stay out late? Maybe we'll see you after the show." There was a painful pause. I felt like a guest who'd stayed too long. They had their plans, and I was this weird stranger they'd met on the plane.

"Don't worry about it," I said lightly. "You guys have fun. Maybe we'll see each other tomorrow. I mean, who knows. I don't want to get in the way."

"No, we can't leave it like that," Katie said. "Why don't we meet somewhere for dinner tomorrow?" I tried to squash a blooming feeling of relief, because if we separated, then I really would be alone in Paris.

We agreed to meet at their hostel the next night at six.

"Have fun," I said. I even sort of meant it.

They left for the show, and I strolled until I found a small café that wasn't too crowded or too empty for me to stand out. There was a large chalkboard with the day's menu scrawled on it. I sat at a table next to two older women and pointed to what they were eating.

"*S'il vous plaît,*" I said. In Paris, it always paid to be polite. The waiter nodded and smiled at me, though not with the same level of adoration of Madison's waiter. I didn't have her tiny, Audrey Hepburn looks. I wasn't fat or squinty-eyed, but I'm curvy, and if I wore baggy shirts, which I tended to because it was easier to blend in that way, I looked heavy. But I couldn't afford to send the wrong message. It paid to play it safe sometimes. Usually. Almost always.

If Peter had been here with me, then when the trip was over, we could tell each other, "We'll always have Paris." I smiled at the thought.

I could see the chef in a kitchen no larger than the one in our apartment in Germany. After I finished most of my meal, I caught his eye and smiled my French smile, the one that said, "I'm not about to make a fool of myself, but this is damn good." He smiled back, nodding self-deprecatingly.

He said something in rapid French to me through the pass-through window.

I smiled but shook my head. There was no use pretending. *"Je ne parle pas français,"* I said, trying my hardest to sound casual and fluent while denying the possibility of a conversation.

"Angleterre?" He thought I was British. Given the French sentiments toward Americans, I decided to accept the offered change in nationality.

"Mm," I said, nodding firmly.

Katie, I noticed earlier, had stitched a Canadian flag to her backpack in hopes of convincing the anti-American world that she was a friendly maple leaf instead of a Texas star. I didn't think much of her tactic but now found myself imitating its intent.

"Ah!" He opened his eyes wide and nodded wisely. "'Arry Potter!" He made a shwooshing movement, I guess to indicate flying, perhaps on a broom.

"Oui." I smiled modestly. "Harry Potter is also British."

Having confirmed this great fact, he nodded again, smiled, and turned to chat with another, more eloquent patron.

I was left alone at the table, swirling the dregs in the wineglass, crumbling a heel of bread into smaller and smaller pieces on my plate. This was my great adventure in Paris. Lovely.

That night, tucked in at the charming Hôtel Jardin by eight-thirty, I couldn't find a comfortable position in bed. But honestly, I wasn't sure if that was because of the lumpy mattress or because of the black hole that sat where my heart used to lie.

If something happened to my mom, I would be alone. No parents. No siblings. Just me. Just me in the dark.

7.

Paris in the morning went a long way to cheering me up. The rattle of grates going up and stores opening, and the smell of fresh bread and pastries, held a delicious promise for a good day. I bought a croissant that was still warm from the oven, then bought a café au lait at a nearby café.

I called some hostels after breakfast. Most were fully booked, but one believed he would have a cancellation by the afternoon and told me to call back. He seemed very confident about the cancellation. When I discovered the Internet café was already open and served coffee, my mood grew even better.

I clicked on my mom's message first.

She was surprised that I was in Paris.

I think it's wonderful, she wrote. *Have fun—eat some chocolate croissants for me and maybe a chocolate crepe or two. And make sure to buy those chocolate circles with the dried fruit on them. Can you tell I miss chocolate? It's not that the food here is bad. It's just not very good. Ha!*

My mom was a huge chocoholic. My dad always bought

chocolates when he went to conferences or business trips and people assumed they were for me, but really, they were for my mom.

Do you remember that bakery we found near the Eiffel Tower, the one with the long line to get in? If you find it again, you have to promise me you'll buy at least three different pastries. Someone in this family should eat well.

The dining hall food isn't bad, she wrote. *It's standard. The eggs are powdered, but I'm used to that. The potatoes are greasy sometimes, dry and crispy other times, and the meat is always a mystery. They say it's chicken, but I have my doubts. It's no worse than the DFAC in Heidelberg. The salad bar is actually decent, and I can tell they're trying hard. So it isn't that the food is so bad, but it repeats. Over and over, the same foods, the same underlying industrial taste. Breakfast, lunch, and dinner. Day after day. Amidst the bizarrely UN-like nature of the base—we've got Danish, Dutch, and British police officers, South African and Ugandan security contractors, Turkish and Serbo-Croatian laundry workers, Filipino maids, Sri Lankan and Indian DFAC servers—you'd think maybe the food would be interesting. I guess that's asking a bit much. Plus, for some reason, they keep running out of forks. Have you ever tried eating salad with a spoon? It's very difficult. We keep joking about a bomb hitting the fork truck. And the hours are horrible—by the time I'm off my shift, the dining hall is usually closed. And then my only options are the fast-food joints by the PX or the instant oatmeal I have in my trailer.*

Honey, I can't wait to take you out to that tiny, ridiculously expensive gourmet place in downtown Heidelberg. I want the seared tuna with mango salsa. I want you to order the roasted, free-range chicken so I can eat that too and thick flourless chocolate cake for dessert. God, I miss sushi!

And the worst part is that I've gained weight. Tell me that isn't adding injury to insult. It's over a hundred degrees, I'm working twelve-hour shifts, I don't have any appetite, but I'm gaining weight. . . . That's so unfair.

Don't mind me. It's the heat. I think I'm having hallucinations. I hope you're having a très bon *time in Paris.*

If you need more money, let me know. I can always transfer you some. I want you to have a good time, sweetie.

I miss you so much.

Love, Mom

Unexpected tears of homesickness welled up, and I blinked quickly to make them go away. I swiped a hand across my nose. My mother. My mother was wonderful.

After I finished writing my mom back, I hit SEND and then settled back with a smile to read Peter's e-mail.

Holy shit, Arden, his message started. *Talk about overshadowing my lame brush with celebrity. You did that just to make me feel like a loser, didn't you?* I grinned at the screen. *But your plan failed. Like I'm going to be jealous that you're spending time with cheese-eating surrender monkeys. Did I mention that George Clooney said hi to me? We're practically buddies. Just do me a favor, don't eat any roasted brains or cow marrow—and don't tell me Frenchies don't eat that because I've seen the shit in my mom's French cookbooks. It doesn't have to be human for it to be cannibalism.*

I tried not to laugh out loud, but as it was, my snorts drew a couple of stares.

But they were delicious, I typed back. *The brains were a little scary at first, but once you get past the texture, they're wonderful. Kind of like soggy chicken.*

I hit SEND, grinning like a fool.

These were the times when I thought back to graduation night and wished things would have turned out differently.

Wished that I were the kind of girl who would seize the moment, never mind the consequences.

But it was better this way, better to have him as a friend than lose him as a boyfriend.

I plotted out the rest of my day. The first goal was to spend as little money as possible. I needed to atone for yesterday. Despite my mom's offer of more money, I didn't feel right taking any from her. Paying for college was already putting a strain on her finances. My impulsiveness shouldn't cost her more.

The plan for the day was that I'd splurge and go to the Louvre but save money by buying my food from a bakery and walking whenever possible. Because, in the words of Lola, you can't come to Paris and not go to the Louvre. Ze French, zey would arrest me.

While my purloined guidebook had a small map of Paris, it was absolutely useless. According to that map, there were about four major boulevards in Paris and nice blank spaces between them instead of the messy twists and turns of alleys and lanes.

Asking for directions was easy. I said, "Louvre?" Everyone knew what I meant, except for one person who pretended she didn't understand. But while getting (most) people to understand where I wanted to go was easy, I couldn't understand their answers. I tried to follow the way their hands were pointing, like if they made that "keep going straight" sort of hand motion or if they curved their hand to the right or the left like an imitation of a swimming fish, but mostly it meant that I kept walking and kept getting lost.

By the time I spotted that famous glass pyramid that is the entrance to the Louvre, it was after ten, I was hot and sweaty, and my feet were sore. Also, the line to buy the tickets stretched out far into the courtyard. With a sigh, I found the end and joined it.

It was nearly noon by the time I paid and walked in. I hadn't counted on the fact that it was four hours since I'd eaten and I was hungry again. I peeked at the museum café, but it was too pricey.

Still, the museum was a glorious place. I soaked in the ambiance of endless marble floors, huge empty rooms with high ceilings, and nothing there but the most brilliant art of the past millennium. It was a palace. An empty palace save for its walls, which were covered in gilded frames, each holding a painting worth more than most people would earn in a lifetime.

It occurred to me that over the course of four hundred years, people had basically stopped living in palaces. With a few notable exceptions, like the queen of England, the ancient ruling aristocracy was gone and in their palaces we'd put art. There was something beautiful about that. As if only art, in its pure sense, deserved such a fine home. As if only art could live in such an opulent, perfect place. Art encased in art, art to complement art.

I found the *Venus de Milo* and the *Winged Victory*, armless and headless and still so beautiful I stopped in my tracks on the stairs, ignoring the masses that bumped past me.

Nine years after my first visit to the Louvre, it was like visiting another place altogether. The beauty and grace of the statues alone made me wonder if I should have had my eyes checked when I was ten; how could I have missed that?

The *Mona Lisa* was a huge disappointment. It was small, and the massive crowds around her made it impossible for me to get more than a glimpse of her famous smile. I wobbled on my tiptoes, craning my head over the shoulders of the people packed in front of me.

There was something there in her smile; I could tell even in the distance. But it seemed that she was laughing at me and I didn't like it.

"Well, gosh, Betty," said one potbellied, red-faced man to his frighteningly similar-looking wife. "It sure looks small, don't it?"

"I did think it'd be bigger," she said.

"Well, there you are," he said. "I guess it isn't just portion size that's smaller in France."

They both sniggered.

I looked around, wondering if there were French tourists who could hear this. I gave up my spot in front of the *Mona Lisa* and walked away, distancing myself from them physically, if not nationally.

"Portraits can tell a story," my dad had said when we were here nine years ago. He pulled me to a stop in front of Hyacinthe Rigaud's famous portrait of Louis XIV.

I looked skeptically at the pasty-looking man in high heels, thigh-high white tights, and long black curls.

"What is this supposed to say: 'here is a stupid-looking man'?"

"*Au contraire*," my dad said. "You're looking at France's greatest, most powerful monarch."

"Really?"

He did have a big sword on his left hip, but he looked too overdressed and too fat to do anything kingly with it.

"He was the definition of the absolute ruler, Arden," my

dad said. "And the portrait couldn't make it clearer. Look how the heavy red and gold drapery behind him creates a frame for his cape," he explained, his hand following the lines of the heavy curtain in the upper-right-hand corner of the frame. "Notice how the cape makes a triangle and he's at the top."

He drew my attention to the thick ermine-lined robe. It looked so soft and plush that I curled my fingers into my palms to keep from reaching out to touch the centuries-old paint. The fleurs-de-lis on the cape were echoed in the upholstering of the throne and footstool next to him, which his crown was on. The fleur-de-lis was the symbol of his family, the House of Bourbon.

"Did you notice his expression?" my dad prodded.

"He looks mean," I said. "And constipated."

"I don't think he looks mean, but it's not a kind expression," he agreed. "The closed lips are meant to look decisive even though his pose is welcoming. But that's on purpose. He's not meant to be kind. Remember, this is a king who was supposed to be divine. He called himself the Sun King and was so above everyone else that wiping his bottom for him was an honor; can you imagine?"

"Ew!" I squealed on cue.

My dad laughed and touched my hair softly. I leaned against him and he put his arm around me as he gazed at the portrait some more.

"When he died, he had ruled France for seventy-two years. Can you imagine that? He was a king from the time he was five years old."

I looked again at the heavyset, dandified man in the painting. Maybe there was something steely in his gaze after all.

* * *

As I left the Louvre, I saw that unbeknownst to me during the time I spent inside the museum, clouds had moved in on Paris. The skies opened up and I dashed through the rain to the nearest open shop.

The shop turned out to be an antique bookseller. Of course, the books were in French, with a smattering here and there in German. The shopkeeper glanced up from his magazine, eyed me and my dripping state. Without saying a word, he managed to convey the message that I was not to drip on the merchandise.

I perused the dusty, musty shelves, picking up a book at random and flipping through its pages, pretending I had some business here. I actually felt a small wave of homesickness when I realized the book I was flipping through had been printed in Heidelberg. It had been published in 1963, the year my father was born, and I caught myself actually looking for the price because it seemed like an omen. But I stopped because what would I do with a three-hundred-page book written in German?

I couldn't get my mom's e-mail out of my head. I wondered if she'd ever see Paris again. Then, catching myself, I forcibly cut off that line of thinking. Nothing would happen to her. Nothing could happen. Medical staff were safe.

Not necessarily, said the little voice that never shut up. A roadside bomb didn't care if there was a large red cross painted on the truck. Suicide bombers didn't ask bystanders their occupation before they exploded; mortars didn't care where they fell and exploded.

After twenty minutes, the rain stopped and I eased out of the shop, peering out at the damp, steaming streets. The clouds had cleared away, and the sun reflected off the puddles with sudden intensity. As if a cease-fire had been declared, civilians emerged from shelters, umbrellas were put away, and life returned to Paris. Joggers trotted by on the path along the Seine. The only hint of the rainstorm was the humidity that hung in the air as the wet ground slowly dried and the puddles evaporated.

I bought lunch from a vendor's cart—a soggy tuna sandwich, heavy with mayonnaise, and a small Coke—cheaper than going into a café. Who needed a table and chair in a dark little restaurant when Paris was one giant picnic site?

I joined the promenade of tourists and locals and followed the river until it led me to the Île de la Cité, the island plot of Notre Dame.

From behind, the supporting buttresses of the cathedral looked like the exposed ribs of some emaciated giant. Feeling spooked by the dark Gothic goliath, I walked around and arrived at the courtyard in front. It was packed with families, tourists, and pigeons. Here the two towers and the familiar rose window seemed more peaceful.

I sat on the low gray stone fence encircling some hedges, sighing in relief like an old woman to be off my aching feet. I listened to kids whine that they wanted ice cream and watched couples hold hands. Eventually my eyes drifted past the impressive front door and its arching design to the top of the cathedral and its famous gargoyles.

It must have been a comfort in some ways to live in a time when Europe was Catholic and everyone believed in God and heaven. I'd once read that in the fourteenth century, twenty-five percent of city budgets in France and Italy were spent on building cathedrals. I wasn't sure if that had any kind of proportional relationship to a level of faith, but it seemed to at least indicate a high degree of confidence in the existence of God. I doubt you'd spend that much on the glory of something you weren't a hundred percent sure existed. Would the church have had so much power without its terrifying ability to excommunicate?

I was Jewish, though growing up in a military community, I'd been surrounded by Evangelicals, Baptists, and born-again Christians. I didn't know what I believed. I wondered about people who were willing to die, to be tortured, because of their belief in God. The great schism that we learned about at school. Martin Luther and the Reformation. The Thirty Years' War. The Crusades. The Holocaust. Europeans in the past had an excess of both faith and murderous conviction. Now, of course, that fervor had shifted to the Middle East, to suicide bombers and calls for jihad. I wondered why faith and killing so often went together. I wondered what gave people that confidence.

I wondered where my dad was, if his spirit could look down and see me. Could he spread his wings over me and keep me safe? Had my dad even believed in heaven? Could you get there if you didn't believe it existed?

Did we have souls?

Did anything survive our bodies when we died?

It was eerie to think of the thousands, the millions of people who had come to Notre Dame to pray, beg, and sightsee who were now dead and gone. The world kept going. Notre Dame was still here, and there were millions more in their place, praying, begging, sightseeing.

With my background, my nomadic existence, I had left an even lighter footprint than most. Maybe that's what happened when you always blended in with the crowd.

I had written Peter about it once, after a spat with my roommate found me tucked away in a corner of the library feeling miserable and lonely. My mom had recently received her deployment orders, and the date seemed like a looming execution. The fight with my roommate had blossomed in my mind into the end of our placid coexistence, the end of my room as a place I could go to except for sleep.

Sometimes I pretended to Peter that I loved college, that being back in the States was great. Mostly because I felt that he loved college and it was lame not to love it. But I also knew that he was the person who would understand what I was talking about.

Do you think because we grew up military, we'll never have a place to call our own? I asked him from the eerie blue glow of the library's computer lab. *We've never had roots growing up. What if we're never able to grow them?*

There wasn't any doubt whom I would e-mail when a black mood rolled in.

No, Arden, you're looking at it from the wrong perspective, he wrote back a few minutes later. *Our childhood gave us unlimited possibilities. Unlike most people, we aren't scared of change, of different places and new people. Think of how many people you know at college where this is the first time they've been anywhere but their hometown. Think how sheltered they've been. Us military brats, we're prepared for anything. A crappy apartment, a deployment, a midyear move, we've been there and we know it might be hard, but we'll get through it and probably find something fun along the way.*

It's crippling to be scared of change, he wrote. *Everything about life changes, all the time. If you're scared of change, it means you're scared of life.*

Reading his answer and feeling my heart nearly ache with the sweetness of it, I finally admitted to myself that what I felt for Peter was more than friendship and a lot closer to love. But I couldn't bring myself to tell him. I could bare my soul to him but not my heart.

I sat in front of Notre Dame for a long time, reluctant to leave the church grounds. I watched as one elderly woman—wearing a knitted cardigan even though it was hot—slowly, painfully climbed the steps to the church and disappeared into the interior gloom.

How much did my mom really share? How much could she share? How could she explain what life was like there? It was a life lived on caffeine, stress, and adrenaline. It was a life full of blood and gore and tears. It was a life of miraculous saves and heart-wrenching losses.

Certain topics were off-limits; some things were classified. I wondered if I would ever really know what my mother was going through. I read as much as I could. There was a whole community of military bloggers. I read about their daily aggravations, about going on patrol, but that wasn't what my mom's life was really like.

As difficult as her life was right now, when she came back, would life seem dull?

How could heart attacks and sliced fingers and the occasional stabbing wound compare? How could being near me compare to the heart-pumping adrenaline thrill of saving so many lives, of being so needed? Right or wrong, the reason for the war in Iraq ceased to matter after a while. Most of the mil bloggers agreed. What mattered was that your buddies were there, and even if they were at the gates of hell or ready to storm the gates of heaven, you would be there with them, watching their backs.

My mom saw the ones who wouldn't live through, the ones who were broken forever, and I worried that it would change her.

When the bells of the great cathedral began pealing, it finally occurred to me that I should have called by now to see if there had been any cancellations at the hostel.

It was later now, nearly four, and he had told me to call by two. I found a pay phone and called, but of course there was nothing available. I was faced with another night at the horrible Jardin.

I rubbed my temple, fighting the beginnings of a headache.

The Seine looked muddy after the rain, but the tourist boats that floated up and down looked sweet, and I wished I could afford to ride one. It seemed my time in Paris was continually spent with my nose pressed up against the window.

I sat on a bench for a while, marking off the time until six, when I'd go meet Katie and the rest. The sun glinted off the tiny ripples in the river, so that they looked like flecks of gold, floating in the water.

I was traveling in Paris. I'd met some new friends. I reminded myself of all the positive things I had to keep me busy.

I'd climbed the ladder to the dive platform; I couldn't climb back down. But that didn't mean I should look down.

I reminded myself of that each time I thought of my dad. Each time I imagined the news, the call that something had happened to my mom.

Don't borrow trouble. Don't look down.

8.

The woman who killed my dad was not a bad person.

She'd just forgotten about that yield-to-the-right rule. She was going the speed limit but driving a 2001 Suburban, a car considered big in the States and gargantuan in Europe. My father was also going the speed limit, but he was driving a 1987 BMW 327i two-door coupe.

We'd bought it for a thousand dollars from a lieutenant PCS'ing, his military orders sending him back to the States. The army paid to ship our minivan from Texas but not our other car, so when we arrived in Germany, we did what everyone else does: buy some German-made hoopty that had over a hundred thousand miles on it but would still run for another hundred thousand miles.

My dad loved that car.

If the proverbial garage were burning and he had to run in and save only one car, there's no doubt in my mind it would be the jalopy that he'd save and not our pricey minivan. The BMW, almost as old as I was, ran better and faster than anything he'd ever driven before. He'd marvel at the tight steering, the acceleration, the response of the car to his slightest whim. There was serious talk between my parents about splurging at the end of our tour and buying a new Beemer to take back home.

My dad wasn't a car guy. He wasn't one of those guys who'd tinker with the engine over the weekend, fuss over the car like a baby. Until we moved to Germany and bought that BMW, he'd never used the car-wash kit we bought him for Father's Day. But he loved that car.

I wonder about that.

I wonder if there was some sort of connection somehow. If he knew he needed to take care of that car because his life was on the line. But that doesn't make sense. If anything, he should have hated that car, feared it. If there's any such thing as premonitions or a sixth sense, then we all should have insisted he buy some giant Mercedes or, even better, a Hummer, the kind with a giant grill in the front that could plow through a cement barrier and be okay.

Because while the little two-door BMW could have danced circles around the hulking Suburban, like a gnat buzzing around a bear, in a crash it didn't stand a chance.

My father, coming in from the right, followed the German driving law, which said he didn't need to slow down for cars coming in from the left. He had the right of way and he sailed through, confident in German traffic obedience.

The woman, Diane Fowelly, had been in Germany for almost two years and never had so much as a speeding ticket. But she usually drove around the post, which suspended the German yield laws. She screamed when she saw a car running the intersection in front of her. She hit the brakes. You could see the skid marks for over a year after the accident. It slowed her enough that she T-ed into the BMW, slamming right into the driver-side door.

My father died instantly. Her fender was barely bent.

The German police investigated since there was a death. But in the end, though she was clearly at fault and had to pay a large fine, there was no criminal intent or gross negligence on her part. It was an accident.

Diane was the one who called the police and the ambulance. She stayed with my father until they got there and then she collapsed, sobbing. In the weeks and months that followed, she refused to drive on German roads, and last I'd heard, her family was given a compassionate reassignment back to the States. Through the military nurses' grapevine my mom found out that almost a year after the accident, Diane was still on Prozac.

In the days and weeks that followed the accident, everyone kept saying that my dad didn't suffer. That he was lucky. He died instantly and didn't ever know what hit him.

I heard it again and again. "At least he didn't suffer." Usually this phrase was accompanied with a heavy hand on my shoulder and a slight squeeze to let me know that the teller shared my pain. I'd be forced to smile and nod, like we were discussing a pair of shoes that were on sale. Yeah, they're ugly, but at least they're fifty percent off.

Of course I didn't want my dad to have suffered. If he had to die, then I wanted it to happen without any pain or suffering. But I wondered if they were right. I wondered what "instantly" meant. For months afterward, I'd find myself going through the accident in my mind at the oddest times. During class or in the middle of conversations, something would trigger a thought and the accident would play through my mind like a movie. Everything I knew, every fact I gleaned, went into directing my father's final moments. People loathed to tell me the details, but I had to know. I'd hunt down any speck of information I could get. How long the skid marks were, how wide, the weight in tonnage of the SUV, of the BMW, the speed on impact. I wanted to know what they did with the mangled hull of the car. Did it go to the junkyard? Was it sold for scrap? I wanted to see it, but my mother wouldn't let me. I wanted to know if the reason she didn't want me to was because there was blood. She finally lost her temper and snapped, "What do you think?"

I stopped asking her questions after that.

I know he must have seen the SUV coming. He must have tried to hit the gas and zip past her. My father had very fast reflexes. I think he probably heard the window shatter. I can't decide if he felt the car frame buckling under the impact. He might have.

You can know a lot in an instant.

My dad always said that's how long it took him to fall in love with my mom. When I was born, in an instant, he said, his whole world changed and he was filled with love to the brim. So maybe it makes an awful kind of sense that that's how he passed from living to dead. Maybe he only needed an instant to figure out the really important things. Maybe he did skip past pain. And even if he had time to be scared, at least he wasn't scared for long.

The thought was a small comfort. But small comforts were all I had.

9.

At six, I entered the hostel lobby and looked around for the three girls. There was a thin guy on a cell phone—I'd guess German—a blond girl writing in a journal—maybe Australian—and two other girls talking in some kind of Slavic language I couldn't place, either Polish or Czech, I thought.

I sat down on one of the hard couches by the door, prepared to wait.

Twenty minutes later, I was reconsidering my options. I'd decided to give up and leave when they spilled in from upstairs.

"Arden! Were you here since six? *Zut alors!* We thought you'd come up."

"I just got here," I lied. "How was Versailles?"

"*C'est formidable!*" Lola said. "I would die to live in a place like that."

"Madison gave us a crash course in French exclamations," Katie filled me in. "We now know *sacrebleu, zut alors*, and *c'est formidable*, if you didn't notice."

"Long train ride to Versailles, huh?"

"Something like that," Katie said. "Versailles was totally worth the trip. But it's so arrogant, you know? To have the nerve to think you deserved something like that? The king's bed was behind this railing that looked like a Communion rail. And it cost like two billion dollars a year in today's money just to maintain Versailles."

"All right, fount of information," Lola cut her off. "Let's tell Arden about the real highlight of the day."

They were talking over each other, Katie telling me about the paintings and the huge gardens and Lola about the three Swedish guys who had lunch with them.

"They speak, like, seven languages."

"Louis the Fourteenth had bankrupted the whole country building his palaces."

"So cute."

I was struck by how full and exciting their day had been. Mine was so quiet and sad in comparison. They weren't scared to be loud, to have fun, to talk to new people.

"How was your day, Arden?" Katie asked.

"It was great," I said, trying to spin it. "What's not to love about Paris? I made it to the Louvre and Notre Dame. . . . It's so calm and peaceful there."

"I'm starving, you guys," Madison said. I was grateful for the interruption. "I'm sorry, but I'm going to pass out if I don't get something to eat. Can we go, please?"

We left the hostel and headed toward a restaurant that Katie had read was good.

When we found it, however, the windows were dark and the door locked. It wouldn't open until seven.

"I'm going to pass out," Madison said. She looked pale, and there was a sheen of sweat on her upper lip. "What's wrong with people here? You can't get lunch after two-thirty? You can't eat before seven? What the hell?"

Katie looked as if it were her fault the restaurant was closed. Madison's skin had turned greenish yellow.

"We can go to a trattoria or charcuterie," I suggested. "They're like snack shops. They're open all day. There's no place to eat in the store; you take the food to go. But it's already made, so it's quick."

"That's a great idea," Katie said in relief.

"Fine, whatever. I *have* to eat."

Charcuteries served as a kitchen away from home for many Parisians. They sold cooked meats, hot and cold prepared dishes, wine, cheeses, fresh breads, pâtés, quiches, salads, even Asian foods like spring rolls and pot stickers, all to go. We entered a shop that had counters full of prepared salads, roasted meats, and side dishes. The prices were affordable, even with the lousy exchange rate that ate up my dollars like some mythical beast Hercules would challenge. With the setup being as it was, it meant we could see what the dishes looked like, know the prices ahead of time, and pick something that both looked good to eat and didn't cost too much.

We took our food to the nearby Luxembourg Garden, walking past a miniature sculpture of the Statue of Liberty given to the city of Paris by the original sculptor, Bartholdi. We picked a bench along a pale gravel path lined with trees. Two old men in caps played chess nearby.

"Great call, Arden," Lola said, winding down with her feast. "This was freaking awesome."

"It's hard until you figure out these little tricks," I said. "My aunt was a tour guide for a while. She said you always had to make sure people can get to food, drink, and a bathroom or they couldn't have fun."

"That is so true. Kind of sad, but true," Madison said sheepishly. "I feel so much better."

Lola handed me the bottle of wine that we'd been passing around. I took a long sip.

"I thought about you today when I heard the news," Katie said as I handed her the bottle.

"The news?"

"Yeah. From Iraq."

"What?" My face heated up, my heart started to race. "What are you talking about?"

"Oh, Arden. You didn't hear about it? I thought for sure you'd have heard—" She broke off, looking nervous and awkward.

"Katie," I said slowly. "What happened?"

"There were seven soldiers killed in a roadside bombing. One of them was a woman. But it couldn't have been your mom. Because she's a nurse and you told me they aren't in as much danger. Right?"

"Where?"

"What?"

"Where was the bombing?" I spoke slowly, and I must have sounded normal because she didn't notice that I was finding it hard to keep down my dinner.

"I don't remember. Lola, Madison, do you guys remember where the bombing was?"

"No," Lola said with a sigh. "That stuff is so awful. I hate thinking about it."

"I think it was Mosul?" Madison said, anxious to help. "Fallujah? They all sort of sound the same. I'm not sure."

I couldn't breathe. I stood up without realizing it. My mom was stationed at the 31st Combat Support Hospital in Baghdad. Could it have been there? Could she have been going somewhere in a convoy? She'd been in one before.

"Are you okay?" Katie stood up, swaying slightly. The wine bottle was nearly empty.

"I have to go," I said, hardly knowing what I was saying. "I have to check my e-mail."

"We'll come with you," Katie said. The other two stood. "You shouldn't be alone."

I shook off an unwanted hand from my shoulder.

"Arden, look at me," Madison said.

I looked.

"Your mom is fine. She's fine. You have to believe that."

"I know." I nodded. "I know she is. I just have to check my e-mail."

I found an Internet café, the three of them tagging along behind me. My heart racing, my thoughts formlessly begging for a message, I logged on.

I don't know if you heard, but there were heavy casualties today, she wrote. *I'm fine, but I don't have time to write more, sweetie, I'm sorry. I knew you'd worry. Now go have fun. Love, Mom.*

My hands started shaking, my knee twitching up and down almost uncontrollably.

"She's okay," I said softly. "She's okay." She didn't have time to write more because she was a nurse and there were wounded.

"Thank God," Lola said.

"Yeah," I echoed. "Thank God."

I was lucky, but there were seven families today who weren't.

The thought of how close I stood to the lip of the cliff, how little separated me from being an orphan, from losing my mom to those foreign, distant sands, sent a wave of prickly heat across my face and made my fingertips tingle.

I don't want to be alone, I thought. *Please, don't let me be the only one left.*

10.

"What should we do now?" Lola asked as we trooped out of the Internet café into the bustling street.

"The jet lag is hitting me hard," Madison said. "Would it be really pathetic to go back to the hostel?"

Visions of my room at the Jardin floated by.

"How about we go to a bar?" I said, a little too quickly.

"That'd be fun," Lola said. "Don't be a party pooper, Madison. It's way too early to call it a night, right, Katie?"

Katie did look tired herself, but she looked at me and then at Lola's eager face.

"One drink," she said.

The bar was packed with an after-work crowd. Smoke drifted in a low cloud above our heads, turning the light slightly blue.

Lola bummed a cigarette off a French guy and smoked it. Madison looked at her with hungry eyes. Lola took a few puffs, but after Katie elbowed her in the ribs, she ground it out in the ashtray on the counter.

We ordered sparkling wine.

"Cheers, y'all," Lola sang out. "To trips with friends!" We clinked glasses.

"To new friends and old friends!" We clinked.

"To Paris!" We clinked.

I was about say, "To good news," but stopped myself because it wasn't good news that seven soldiers had been killed.

Madison had a glass, but aside from taking one tiny sip, she didn't drink from it; it was more of a prop than a drink. I was getting ready to ask if something was wrong, but then two French guys joined our small table.

"*Bonjour,*" Lola said in a low purr. I stopped myself from correcting her that it was "*bonsoir*" since it was nighttime. I noticed that the French guys didn't care.

Fortunately, they spoke some English.

"Where are you from?" the one with rimless glasses asked.

"Canada," Madison said before any of us could answer. "We're all Canadians. Did you think we were Americans?"

"*Non, non.*" They both shook their heads in denial.

Lola and Madison giggled.

Katie hadn't joined Lola and Madison's French flirtations. Instead, looking a little sad, she toyed with her glass. "This is what it's going to be like if Jack deploys, isn't it?" she asked me softly.

"Yeah," I said, resisting the urge to sugarcoat the truth. "Pretty much. Sucks, huh?"

"It's awful," she said. "How much longer is she going to be there?"

"She should be back around Christmas, if they don't extend her tour."

"They can do that?"

"It's the army," I said. "They can do anything they want."

Suddenly I felt the weight of jet lag, a deep weariness and heaviness pulling me down. I wanted to believe that God or fate or whatever was up there deciding who lives wouldn't, couldn't take my mother. But I knew the futility of thinking like that. There wasn't anyone keeping score. No one with a clipboard making sure the outcome was fair.

By nine, I told them I needed to go. Nothing was funny; the smoke was too thick, the laughter too loud. We agreed to meet the next morning.

I walked back to my hotel, not caring that it was a forty-minute walk. I needed to clear my head. My feet were mostly steady, but I'd had more wine in the past three hours than the past three years. It dulled everything. Except for longing. It sharpened that into the burning point of a laser. Nobody told me alcohol could do that.

All I could think about was the house in Sardinia. Its white walls that stayed cool to the touch no matter how hot it was outside. Its small porch that dangled off the edge of the mountain, looking down to the ocean. The kitchen and my parents' bedroom were on the ground floor. My bedroom was upstairs next to the bathroom. My room had bunk beds, and I always slept in the top bunk near the window. I would fall asleep with my fingertips on the glass pane, the night and the stars on the other side.

In the mornings, we'd let my mom sleep in.

I'd come down the steps on tiptoes. My dad, an early riser, was always on the porch by then. I'd find him sipping his first cup of coffee as he watched the ocean below. It was still a bit cool in the morning, and there was always a breeze on the porch. I would shiver in my thin shirt and savor the goose bumps spreading on my arms and legs. By early afternoon, the sun would be scorching.

"*Buon giorno, principessa,*" my father would say in an expansive Italian accent. I'd lean in for a kiss, and his warm breath, smelling of coffee, started my day.

"Are you ready?" he'd ask, and I'd nod.

We'd sneak out of the house, taking care to close the door quietly behind us. Then we'd walk down the hill, past all the other quiet houses, to the café. It was always quiet in the mornings. Even at nine, hardly anyone stirred.

There was a large fig tree that grew next to the café, shading the porch. Sometimes I would pick a handlike leaf and pretend to give my dad a high five. Inside, the café was so full of the smell of sweet coffee that I could smell it on my shirt for hours afterward.

"What'll it be?" my dad would ask. This was our ritual. "Cappuccino?"

"No."

"Espresso?"

"Nope."

"*Grappa?*" he'd ask in horror. *Grappa* was a clear, harsh alcoholic drink that some weathered old men drank a shot of for breakfast.

"No," I'd giggle. Even the last time we were there, when I was sixteen, I still found it funny, although I rolled my eyes, too cool to laugh. "Hot chocolate, please."

"Oh," he'd pretend to remember. "That's right. The usual."

After he placed our orders, hot chocolate for me and an espresso for him, I'd stand on my tiptoes and inspect the day's pastry selection. I'd pick out one for me, one for him, and one to bring home to my mom.

We'd take our pastries and our drinks to a corner table and watch the other early risers come in for their caffeine fix. Sometimes my mother's pastry didn't make it out the door.

"Here," my dad would say, handing me a bill. "Go pick out another one. It'll be our secret."

When I'd go to the counter and order another pastry, the proprietress would laugh and shoot my father an amused look.

"*Buono, no?*" It's good, right?

"*Sì,*" he'd reply. "*Troppo buono.*" Too good. Then we'd stroll back to the house.

Usually we'd make it out of the house by noon or one and join everyone else down at the beaches. The sun would be so hot, the rough sand hurt to walk on. When I was younger, my dad would carry me to our blanket. As I grew older and too big to be carried, I would hop from one foot to the other, bypassing the blanket and heading straight to the water. Wet feet didn't burn on the sand like dry feet.

My mom would bring fruit and bread for lunch. The grapes would burst sweetness into my salty mouth. The lukewarm water would taste cool in my thirst. She and my dad would lie on the blanket and fall asleep, their hands touching, while I explored the tall, jagged rocks with names like Eagle's Head and the Brontosaurus, always giggling when I saw the one named "the Penis." There'd be other Italian teenagers playing around and I'd join them, the only blonde in a sea of bobbing black heads. What little Italian I knew I picked up from them.

I wanted it to be then.

Forget Paris with its gray stone palaces, its narrow streets and wet roads. I wanted to be on a desert island with a brutally hot sun and dry crumbly earth, scrub grass, and stunted trees. I wanted to see the ocean sparkle like the world's largest aquamarine jewel and my parents asleep on the sand holding hands.

As fierce as my desire was, it was hopeless.

The place I wanted to go to didn't exist anymore. My dad

wouldn't be there with me to buy pastries for breakfast. My mom wouldn't be there to wake up with a sleepy smile at the smell of cappuccino coming off our clothes and a grease-stained bag with a chocolate-filled *cornetto*. The house, after this summer, wouldn't be ours to use again. Maybe it didn't matter, in the end, that we were selling it.

The place I wanted to go to was a memory.

Unable to face my hotel just yet, I went to another Internet café and bought a half hour. Before I knew it, I was on Hotmail, e-mailing Peter.

I just had a horrible scare, I wrote him. *It's hard being out of touch here in Europe. I haven't seen the news since I got here. I check my e-mail once a day, but bad things are always happening over there and I miss not knowing what's happening. On the one hand, it's kind of nice. It's easier to put it out of my mind. Almost like the situation in Iraq doesn't exist. But then I remember that it does, and not knowing what's going on is ten times scarier than watching the news 24/7.*

Do you still have feelings for me? I wanted to write. *There was that night after graduation; do you still think about it?* But I didn't write that because I never mentioned it to him or he to me. I knew he cared for me as a friend; I also knew I wanted more.

I can't decide what to do about these girls I'm traveling with. There's a part of me that's dying to get back to Sardinia. I love it there so much. But I guess I worry that when I get there, it'll be awful. When I'm with the Texans, it's so much easier not to think about it. We're your typical ugly Americans, straight out of those awful AFN, the military-run television network, commercials. We laugh too loud, we make fun of people, we stick out in a crowd. I love it. I love you.

I know I'm only putting off the inevitable. But I feel like I'm entitled to some fun this summer. And maybe this is the best chance at fun I'm going to have.

I made it back to my hotel, filled with a painful sense of disappointment. The elation of knowing my mom was unhurt had faded; the horrible fear that she could have been hurt lingered. Things changed so quickly.

The clerk behind the counter looked up suspiciously as I entered.

"What room are you staying at?" he asked, eyes narrowed. Considering the type of neighborhood the hotel was in, I supposed it wasn't an unreasonable question. But coming after such a bad evening and on top of the fact that I already resented paying so much for the room, the question infuriated me.

"Room 507," I said, and fished out my key, dangling it in front of him.

"You are not supposed to leave with the key!"

"What?"

"You are not supposed to leave with the key," he repeated. "When you leave the hotel, you must leave it at the front desk."

"Fine," I said, clenching my teeth. "I'll do that next time."

He flipped through his records. "You have not paid for tonight. You must pay now." Another fifty-five euros down the drain.

Back in my nasty little room, I sat on the bed with my head in my hands, fighting the urge to bawl like a baby.

Life went on. There were bills to pay, dinner to cook. I still put shoes on before going outside. I still needed to shower and use the bathroom. Who decided this? Who decided which things remained and which things, which wonderful, beautiful things, vanished?

11.

By the third day of Paris sightseeing, we started running out of big-ticket items. We'd seen the Eiffel, the Louvre, the Musée d'Orsay; and we'd walked the Left Bank from one end to the other. We'd eaten stinky cheese, warm baguettes, and chocolate-filled pastries and ordered a café au lait at Café Deux Magots. They'd even paid me back for the RER.

Every day my e-mails to my mom were filled with a gastronomic rundown of what I'd eaten, where I'd bought it, and how wonderful it tasted. Vicarious thrills were the best I could give her. To Peter, I described the awful cheese course we ordered at a recommended bistro.

It was Lola's idea to order the cheese course.

"It's very European to finish a meal with a cheese course instead of a sweet dessert," she said. We looked at each other and shrugged.

"I'm game," Madison said.

The waiter, a cadaverous-looking man, brought out a chilled pewter platter with five lumps of cheese artistically displayed. He set it down on the middle of our table with a flourish.

Each cheese was coated with a gray-green fuzz of mold and smelled worse than most trash cans.

"Do you think he brought us the leftover rinds no one else would eat?" Katie asked.

I knew Peter would enjoy hearing about that. He'd probably respect me if I told him I ate the whole stinking cheese tray and gave a mighty cheese-smelling belch at the end. Which I didn't, but still.

I think I heard the waiters cracking up in the back, I wrote. *I bet they were taking bets to see if we'd eat it.*

We tried them all because we figured that surely, the next one couldn't be as bad as the one before, I wrote to my mom and to Peter. *But we were wrong. They tasted like freaking toe jam, not that I've ever had any, but you get my point.*

Madison had turned green at the smell and excused herself. Lola joined her after a taste, and we conceded defeat. Katie waved to the waiter to come take the nasty plate away.

Here's what I didn't tell Peter. Determined not to get gypped again since everyone ordered a different-priced meal, I grabbed the bill when it came and started doing the math, trying to figure out how much each person owed. The bill was a messy scrawl, and it took me a while to decipher it.

"Do you remember how much your veal was?" I asked Katie.

"Oh for God's sake," Lola burst out. "I can't stand this." She reached for her wallet and pulled out her credit card. "Fuck it," she said. "Just put it all on my card."

"But you don't have any money," Katie said. "You're broke."

"I know, but I can't stand this."

She paid for the meal. Even though I made it a point to buy

her a crêpe from the crêpe stand we passed and the entry fee to the disco we went to later on, I still felt small. Small and cheap.

On the third day in Paris, there was a cancellation at the hostel and I moved in with the rest of the girls. I probably would have left Paris sooner if Katie hadn't gotten me into the hostel. Hôtel Jardin was starting to wear away at my nerves and my wallet.

Katie asked every morning and evening if there'd been any changes in vacancy. Whether there really had been a cancellation or whether her persistence had finally irritated the receptionist to the point of rearranging sleeping assignments, we never knew. Katie felt wonderfully vindicated and I was grateful for the effort.

"Squeaky wheel gets the grease," she said, looking smug. "Works every time."

How could I leave after that? Besides, I reasoned, I had a month before my return ticket home. What were another few days in Paris?

I spent two nights at the hostel, talking late into the night with the three of them, reveling in being part of a sisterhood of friends.

Paris's gray cobblestone roads, the heavily carved buildings that loomed overhead, the bizarre yet compelling fashion for sale at exorbitant prices were all targets of our jokes, of their camera lenses, and of endless rounds of conversations.

"There's nothing here that Texas can't top," Lola said, her tone half joking and half not.

"How can you say that?" Madison shrieked, drawing glances. We were back at the Eiffel Tower park, watching joggers go by and little children ride a miniature train that chugged in endless circles.

Lola smothered a grin.

"You're not serious," Madison insisted. "There's no city in the world like Paris. Even the air here is different."

"Yeah," Lola said. "It's full of smog and BO."

Katie and I laughed. It was unlikely that our tour guide at the Musée d'Orsay had showered since the Americans liberated the city sixty-five years earlier.

"You might have a point about that," Madison conceded. "But did you notice her dress? It was stunning. And her accent was so cute."

Katie and I left them to their cultural fluency debate as she and I pored over her guidebook to decide where to visit next. But the fact was, there were small neat check marks next to every starred venue. We'd been to all the places she planned for us to see.

"How about an hour at an Internet café?" I suggested.

The one I found was a huge place with several floors. They had a bar that served drinks and light snacks at the ground level near the entrance. As I walked by rows and rows of monitors, I was struck by how many different languages were displayed on the screens. There were people typing away in Russian, French, German, and Japanese, and those were just the few in my range of view.

I read my mom's e-mail and answered her, describing our latest brush with the uniquely Parisian blend of haughty superiority and stunning art, fashion, and food.

When I read Peter's e-mail, I burst out laughing. He had sent me recipes from Julia Child's *Mastering the Art of French Cooking* for cooking brains and baking cucumbers.

Don't let them brainwash you too, he wrote. *The French know squat about cooking. It's an emperor-with-no-clothes syndrome. Just because everyone says the French cook wonderfully doesn't make it true.*

Katie, on a computer one row away, looked up at the sound of my laughter. She walked over and read Peter's e-mail over my shoulder.

"This is the swimmer, right?"

I'd told them about Peter and my unrequited crush. I said way too many things at one in the morning.

"Yeah," I said. "That's the one."

"He has some pretty strong opinions," she said. "Don't tell Madison about the recipes." We both giggled.

I e-mailed Peter back, describing Madison's infatuation with all things French.

Signs of wishful thinking, I queried. *Or evidence of a profound appreciation for aesthetics that the rest of us bourgeois peasants lack?*

Later that afternoon, we sat on a bench in the Rodin garden, watching Madison imitate *The Thinker*. "I think it's time to move on," Katie said once Madison unfurled herself off the boulder she had perched on like a thoughtful bird on a nest. "Where to next?"

"How about Florence?" I said. As soon as I said it, I wondered why. I'd planned to continue straight to Sardinia from Paris. I couldn't seem to stop myself from procrastinating. I wondered if they'd agree. I wondered if this was where we'd part and I'd be forced to continue on my own. I wondered if maybe I needed a kick in the pants to get it over with.

"Sounds good," Lola said.

"Sweet," Madison agreed.

"Do you know when the train leaves?" Katie asked.

And that was that. We weren't going our separate ways quite yet.

The morning we left, I returned the battered guidebook I'd borrowed to the small bookcase in the lobby. Next to the entry recommending Hôtel Jardin, I wrote: "Welcome to our fine hotel, where the sinks double as toilets. Stay at your own risk!"

12.

I had never been to Florence, not in all the times I came to Italy. My parents had talked about it, but we never wanted to cut our time in Sardinia short, not even to see Florence. It had been one of the stops on their honeymoon. I pictured a city with art in its veins, beauty in the very air that flowed in the streets. The last stop on their honeymoon was Sardinia, where they impulsively bought the house, making the down payment with money from their wedding. Nine months later, I came along.

If Paris was a disappointment and Sardinia a terrible chore, then Florence would be my gift to myself, a balm to soothe what ailed me. At least I hoped so.

The train settled into its rocking motion, chugging along toward the Alps.

"Where did you get your name from?" Katie asked as the French countryside whipped by. "Arden is an unusual name, isn't it?"

"Actually, it's from Shakespeare."

"Really? I don't remember a character named Arden," Madison, our resident lit major, said.

"It isn't a character. It's a forest in *As You Like It,* where good things happen, where people can get away from their troubles." I smiled at the irony.

Katie smiled back, without the irony. "I think it's a beautiful name. I was named after my grandmother Kate."

"I'm named after my mother's maiden name," Madison said.

"Well, I top all of you," Lola said. "My parents were hippies. I'm named after that freakin' song. You know, by the Kinks. *Looola, Lo-lo-lo-lo-loooola?*" she sang. Then she glared at us. "I get that it's the first song my parents ever danced to; that sounds pretty romantic. They promised each other that if they ever had a daughter, they'd name her Lola. Except, didn't they listen to the lyrics?"

"Why?" Madison asked.

"Lola's a man!"

"What?" Madison said, startled. "You're wrong."

Lola shot her a look that said she knew what she was talking about, and to prove it, she sang part of the song.

"Well, I'm not dumb, but I can't understand," she sang in a voice surprisingly deep and rich, *"why she walked like a woman and talked like a man. Oh my Lola, Lo-lo-lo-lo-lola."*

We burst out laughing. She raised her hands for quiet and we settled to listen to the rest.

"Well, I'm not the world's most masculine man, but I know what I am and I'm glad I'm a man." She paused dramatically. *"And so is Lola, Lo-lo-lo-lo-lola."*

We cheered and clapped.

"Jesus," Lola said, breaking off the song in disgust. "Who names their child after a transvestite?"

I didn't break the laughter to tell them that the real forest of Arden was based on the Ardennes, where the Battle of the

Bulge took place. Thousands of Americans died there. How would they like to be named after a grave site where thousands of Americans were buried? Seemed like that would give a transvestite a run for his or her money.

A few hours later, the train crossed by the Alps, snow-covered in June.

The conversation turned, as it inevitably did, to my nomadic childhood.

"I don't know that I could have moved around so much as a kid," Katie said to me. "I mean, you never had any continuity, no home base. Every two years you lived someplace new. No kindergarten friends who you grew up with. That must have been tough."

I shrugged and launched into my usual spiel, the one I used anytime I ran across nonmilitary kids I wanted to be friends with.

"Sure, it could it be tough, but I learned to get along with a lot of different types of people, a lot of different situations." I waited a beat. "I can make friends with a hubcap," I said. "If I wanted to."

They laughed, like they were supposed to.

"So tell us about this house in Sardinia," Lola said, keeping the conversation going. "Katie said something about you selling it?"

"Yeah," I said. "It's nothing fancy, a cabin with two bedrooms and one bathroom in this little town called Guspini. It's on a cliff looking over the water. When I was a kid, as soon as I got out of the car and smelled the air there, I'd be happy."

"That sounds beautiful."

"The whole island of Sardinia is beautiful. Full of cliffs and turquoise water that makes you feel like you could float away. Not many Americans visit it, but it's an amazing place. Did you know that native Sardinians have one of the longest life expectancies in the world?"

"Did you say that sardines have a long life expectancy?" Madison asked, coming back from the bathroom.

We all burst out laughing.

"No, dummy," Lola said. "Arden is telling us about Sardinians, the islanders, not the fish."

When I was with the Texans, laughing, it was easier not to worry about all the things waiting for me. Sardinia seemed far away, didn't seem as sad.

"This is kind of boring," Madison said after her fifth trip to the toilet. She looked frailer than usual. Her jaunty nose stud looked out of place on her pale face. "I didn't think we'd be on the train for so long."

"Europe's not as big as the States, but it's big enough," I said.

"Everyone always says how small it is," she said, shoulders up defensively. "How was I supposed to know?"

"Crap, you guys!" Lola shoved her open pack in disgust. "I left my Rainbows at the hostel! Crap!" She hit her bag in frustration.

The train pulled into Florence as the sun was setting. Unlike the Paris station, which was large but modern with lots of skylights and bright colors, the station here felt like it could have been built during the time of the Romans. It had high gray walls, dark marble floors, and tall ceilings with rafters full of pigeons that would come swooping down according to their own sense of drama.

I found an exit and led everyone out of the noisy train station into an even noisier dark street, packed with cars, horns blasting. Hole-in-the-wall cafés spilled customers out into the narrow sidewalk. Mopeds, usually with two riders, wove around the traffic-jammed cars. I had to turn sideways to fit, carrying my pack, through the crowds.

A wafting smell of pizza reminded me my lunch on the train had been expensive and small. I glanced at Madison and saw that she looked a little pale.

"Do you mind if we grab something to eat?" I asked. "That pizza smells amazing."

"Arden, you're saving my life," Madison said.

We all crossed the street, jogging awkwardly with our packs, and entered the first pizza stand I found. I caught Katie and Lola beaming at me in approval.

Up on my toes, I peered at the pizzas under the glass case. The man behind the counter asked me something. I pointed at the cheese pizza and held up two fingers.

He grunted and with two sharp slashes sliced a generous wedge and slid it in the oven.

I handed Madison one of the slices and stepped aside to let Katie and Lola order.

Before I knew it, I was holding the empty white cardboard it'd been served on. Feeling just a bit embarrassed, I returned to the counter and ordered a second one. The man laughed.

"*Buona?*"

"*Sì*," I said. "*Molto buona.*"

"You speak Italian?" Lola asked, breaking into my gluttonous gazes at the pizza counter.

"Sort of," I said. "*Un po'.*" I held my thumb and forefinger an inch apart.

"That's awesome. I thought we'd have to rely on my Spanish to get us through. Did you study Italian in school?"

"No. Just picked it up from the trips to Sardinia. Would anyone want to split another slice with me?"

"Sure," she said, grinning. We walked back to the counter

together. "I got most of my Spanish visiting my relatives in Mexico," she said.

"I wish I could speak another language," Katie said after ordering another slice for her and Madison. "I studied Spanish in school, but it didn't stick."

We finished those slices, and with our bellies full, our brains could resume function.

"So what's the plan?" Madison asked. "Where's this place we're spending the night?"

The day before, Katie and I had braved the European international calling system to book a place for us in Florence. There was no way I was leaving to the last minute again finding a hotel.

"Oh, don't worry about it," Katie said, wiping the orange grease from her lips. "I've got the directions." She opened her purse, flipped open her notebook to the page tabbed Florence, and unclipped a note with a hand-drawn map.

She led us six blocks into the heart of Florence, down streets that seemed too narrow for the amount of traffic that squeezed through. The buildings on either side of the streets were tall with terra-cotta walls and large windows with shutters painted in romantic, peeling shades of green and blue. The cars edging along the paved street nearly brushed us as we walked along a foot-wide sidewalk that we had to share with dozens of other pedestrians. Through this mess, mopeds kept snaking, weaving between parked cars, bicyclists, moving vehicles, and, occasionally, pedestrians.

I surreptitiously breathed in the exhaust, dust, mold, trash, and faint scent of bread that permeated the street. It was great to be in Italy again. The hectic pace was comforting.

With a final glance at her paper, Katie stopped in front of a giant wooden door with metal studs that looked like every other wooden door in front of every other building we'd passed. She scanned the brass buzzer that listed the different floors and pushed down on one of them.

"*Pronto?*" a tinny voice barked at us.

"Hi?" she said. "Is this the Convènto Sacro di Fiore?"

"*Sì.*"

"We have a reservation for four, under Katie Carr."

The sigh was clearly audible through the bad intercom connection. Whatever this place was, an eagerness for guests was clearly not one of its charming habits. There was a long pause, and Madison looked at me and made a face. I had started to say maybe we'd better look elsewhere when the buzzer sounded and the door clicked open.

We entered a cool, dark atrium that had three bicycles with chains around their front tires and a wide staircase made of white marble steps and a wooden handrail that was almost black with age and the countless hands that had brushed against it.

"It's on the fourth floor," Katie said.

There was, of course, no elevator.

We made it to the fourth floor, slightly breathless, and knocked on the unassuming white door. It had a tiny, handwritten sign next to it, proclaiming we had arrived at Convènto Sacro di Fiore. It was only when I saw the words written out that I finally figured out where we were.

"This is a convent?" I exclaimed.

Katie looked at me. "Yeah, why?"

"A convent? We're staying at a convent? With nuns?"

"Yeah," she said, looking at me like I was an idiot. "During the summer they take in guests to make money. But only women."

"I can't stay at a convent."

"Why not?"

"I'm Jewish." That was another thing, like my mother being deployed or my father being dead, that I didn't usually tell people. It wasn't that I thought people were anti-Semitic. It was that it was another barrier to fitting in, another thing to make people think I was different than them. But having blurted it out now, I wasn't sorry. Katie, Lola, and Madison, I was beginning to figure out, could handle a few differences.

"So?"

"I don't know. It doesn't seem right." It didn't. I liked nuns because who wouldn't after seeing *The Sound of Music* or *Sister Act*, but I didn't think they'd want to host a Jew, not unless they were hiding them from Nazis.

"Look," Katie said, exasperated. "I'm not Catholic either. They don't care what your religion is. They won't give you a quiz or make you say a Hail Mary. Besides," she said, pulling out her ace in the hole, "they charge twenty-five euros a night *and* they give breakfast. Try finding *that* anywhere else in this town."

That shut me up.

"Don't worry, Arden," Lola said, grinning and touching the small gold cross around her neck. "I'll protect you."

"Shut up," I muttered, but couldn't help smiling back.

The woman who opened the door wore a pale silk shirt with a lace collar and a tweed skirt that came down to just below her knees. She wore a small gold cross, a lot like Lola's, but there was nothing particularly nunlike about her. She eyed us, especially Madison's low-rise jeans that exposed her pierced navel, but sighed and stepped aside, opening the door wide enough for us to walk through.

My Italian, not great to begin with, was rusty after three years. It took me a while to understand, but eventually I figured out that each room slept two girls. "I'll sleep with Katie," Madison said. "Lola snores."

"I do not!"

With another sigh, the woman led us down a white corridor and showed us the two rooms we could have.

The room Lola and I would share was plain but clean, which counted for a lot in my book. There were two narrow beds up against the walls, two small wooden desks with a shelf above each desk, and one closet.

I dropped my pack by the empty bed next to the window and sat down with a sigh of relief. Clearly, Florence was going to work out much better than Paris.

A moment later, Madison popped her head in.

"You ready?"

"Where are we going?"

"To see the greatest cathedral of all time, of course," she said. "We must see the Duomo di Firenze," she said with an exaggerated Italian accent. It was as awful and funny as her French one.

As we left, the nun indicated the small black-and-white clock on the wall and pointed to eleven to make us understand we had to be back by then.

It wasn't hard to find the Duomo.

I hadn't realized what a massive structure it was until we were walking and I happened to glance down a side alley. All I could see, filling in the entire space at the end of the narrow street, was striped marble and a dome so large I had to crane my neck to see the top of it.

I touched Katie and Lola on the arms to stop them.

"It's that way," I said, pointing.

They followed my finger and gasped.

The cathedral was lit up for the night, and it seemed to glow and float above us. There were, of course, a million tourists clustered around it, like ants buzzing with excitement over a three-layer cake. And like a giant among ants, the Duomo dwarfed us all and rose above us with majestic indifference.

"I take it back," Lola said. "Not everything is bigger in Texas."

The Duomo was made of white, green, and red marble, full of carvings of saints and sinners, popes, priests, gargoyles, and who knew what else.

"I can't believe this was built with no electricity or gas-powered tools or trucks or anything," Katie said. "How is that possible?"

Maybe that's what could be done with the certainty of faith.

The doors were locked, so we couldn't see what the inside looked like, but we walked the circumference of it. All of it was beautiful and massive and glowing.

Because we'd already eaten pizza, and it was dark, and we had a curfew, that was all we did our first night. I think Madison and Lola were ready to do more, but in the end, by ten we were back at the convent like good little Catholic girls. I took a long, hot shower that helped me feel clean for the first time in days.

As Lola and I settled down for bed, I couldn't get over how impressed I was with Katie. She'd never been outside the United States before, and yet she had prepared so well for the trip. She'd picked out a great place in Paris and again in Florence—a cheap place, off the beaten path.

"She is so perfect," I said to Lola. I meant it in a good way, an envious way. "She's so put together and on top of things."

Katie was always dressed in a crisp shirt, no wrinkles, no stains, and her hair was always in place with no frizzies from the humid summer heat.

"Yeah," Lola said, her tone belying her words. "I guess she is." Lola unzipped her pack but didn't unpack. She rummaged until she found her pajamas, and with her back turned to me, she started to get undressed.

"You don't think so?" I asked as I turned away to face the window and give her the privacy she clearly wanted.

"Her mom left when Katie was three."

"A lot of people get divorced." Looking out the window, I watched as a nun rode a bicycle. She skillfully maneuvered around two taxis waiting at the curb, her pedaling smooth and steady. I watched her for a moment illuminated by a streetlight: pale blue habit, thick stockings, orthopedic shoes. Now, that was what a nun was supposed to look like. Her head was slightly bent, watching the road as she rode away. I wondered if she had all the answers.

"No, Aiden. She *left* them." Lola's tone pulled me away from the window. "Katie and her brother, who was like six months old at the time. She left them alone in the house and walked away. She lives in El Paso now and works in a bookstore." She pulled on a large T-shirt and then slipped off her bra, pulling the straps down her arms and removing it without revealing an inch of skin. "She's never come to visit Katie at school, she didn't come to her graduation, nothing. Katie tried to get in touch with her a couple of times and she was nice enough, but each time it was clear she doesn't want anything to do with her kids."

I opened my mouth to say something but realized Lola didn't expect an answer. She tossed a pale peach bra onto the top of her pack.

"You think something like that doesn't mess you up? No one's perfect," she said. "Not even Katie."

She squatted to dig out her toiletry kit and then left to brush her teeth and wash her face. I sat on my bed, thinking about what she'd said. Nothing about Katie showed that she'd had a difficult childhood. It made me wonder what did or didn't show on me. My dad might have left me, but he didn't choose to do so. It gave me a new perspective for how unfair life could be.

Madison had been right. Lola did snore. Exhausted by the long day, she fell asleep within minutes. The room wasn't perfectly dark, the curtain too thin to block the streetlights. It was hot inside, and when I opened the window, the sound of traffic filled the room. As I lay there, however, listening to the soft sounds of Lola sleeping and watching headlights from the cars below arch across the ceiling, I felt at peace.

The history of Jews is that of wanderers. You wouldn't find many massive synagogues made out of stone. In fact, historically, there was only one temple built, then rebuilt after the Babylonians destroyed it. It was destroyed for the second and final time by the Romans, long before Europe turned to Jesus. Instead of cathedrals, we had Torah scrolls, bigger than a bread box, but not by much. A highly portable testament of our beliefs. I understood such measures, but still, sometimes it was nice to see proof of your faith larger than life and permanently on display. Somewhere, not far away in the soft Italian night, the great Duomo stood, a massive testament to the belief that God existed, that He loved us, and that we were not alone. And here I was, in a pocket-sized convent, in a small plain room, with one friend sleeping soundly across the room and two others sleeping softly down the hall. I was glad I had disembarked in Paris.

13.

We had breakfast the next morning in the small dining room with the rest of the girls staying at the convent. Breakfast consisted of a softball-sized poofy roll that pretty much disappeared once you cut it open, leaving you with a mess of crumbs on your plate and two morsels of wispy bread. Two small tins of jams, one pocket of butter, and milky coffee completed the meal. It was free, so I wasn't going to complain, but it wouldn't keep me full for long. Then again, I was in the land of the best food in the world, so maybe getting hungry quickly was an advantage.

"We're in the most beautiful city in the world, with more art in one piazza than some countries have in all their collections put together. But"—Madison lifted a finger and continued in a professorial tone—"the very first thing we *must* do is visit the most beautiful man in all the world."

Lola raised an eyebrow.

"I speak, you heathens, of *David*."

"The statue?" Lola said.

"Just wait, sweetie. Just you wait."

So after breakfast, we went on a date with the world's sexiest statue.

Entering the museum after a thirty-minute wait, we walked down a long, darkened hall, ignoring the other pale statues that lined the walk because there was only one thing to see and it was straight ahead. I stopped dead in my tracks at the lit, nearly glowing statue that stood under a domed skylight.

David was huge, and he was beautiful. He was up on a pedestal nearly ten feet high, so that even his feet, ten perfect toes and nails, were well above everyone's head. As I craned my neck up and up, my eyes traveled past his calves, knees, strong thighs, his privates—exposed to the world but still beautiful— his washboard stomach, broad pecs, muscular arms, until finally I reached his face and felt myself fall in love, just a little bit, with a statue.

The white marble showed every ripple of muscle. His veins seemed to pulse with life; he had the most serene expression of pure peace and beauty on his face. Art scholars called it the greatest statue ever made, and I agreed.

"Jesus, he's gorgeous," I heard Lola say under her breath.

"Yeah," I whispered, eloquent as ever. Peter would look like that, I thought with a blush, if he were naked and made out of marble. I'd been to a swim meet of his when he stood by the pool wearing nothing but a tiny black paper suit that made a Speedo look big, drops of water running down his chest and his legs. I'd almost stopped breathing, and it took me a moment to realize that every other girl in the place had her eye fixed on him, drinking in the sight. I didn't go to any more of his swim meets after that.

After a few minutes, Madison moved on to look at some

other statues and Katie and Lola read the signs describing the renovations being done to preserve *David*, but I stayed put, rooted to the spot. Tourists came and went by me and I ignored them. I felt hypnotized and I finally understood that Greek myth about the sculptor who falls in love with his statue. If you could make something so beautiful, how could anything human, and therefore imperfect, ever compare?

After *David* and I communed for a while, expressing our mutual admiration for one another and the futility of our love, I finally tore myself away from the crowd milling at his feet and explored the rest of the museum, keeping an eye out for the rest of the girls, who'd disappeared.

Apart from *David*, there were several other statues by Michelangelo, and since I was now a fan, I went to look for them. The unfinished *Prisoners*, or *Slaves*, reaffirmed Michelangelo's genius to me. The statues showed men struggling, their faces and arms lifelike in their anguish and pain. The bottom two-thirds of each statue was still only a hunk of raw marble, making the figures look as if they were struggling to get out of the rock. Michelangelo started each of his magnificent statues looking at a lump of dirty white marble and he chiseled out of it something graceful and real. Unlike with painting, if he made a mistake, if he changed his idea even slightly, he couldn't start over. Once the marble was cut or chipped, there was no going back. He couldn't decide that the nose looked a little small and make it bigger, that the arm wasn't proportional and go back and fix it. I couldn't imagine the sort of genius it would take to be a sculptor.

I returned to *David*, stood awhile longer by the glowing white marble. The rotunda surrounding him and the skylight directly above him were the perfect showcase for this statue. It appeared as if the entire museum really had been designed and built around *David*. I couldn't fault them for that.

My father must have loved seeing this when he came here with my mom. It was both beautiful and precise. My mother, too, must have appreciated *David's* beauty. Maybe she and I could come back here. Then again, maybe she wouldn't want to return to the site of her honeymoon without my dad.

The perfection of the human body reminded me of one of the saddest e-mails I ever got from my mom. It was a few weeks into her tour and she'd had a bad day.

The surgery went through thirty units of blood, she wrote. *We started running low and had to get three A-pos. volunteers to donate blood until the medevac could arrive with more units. And it doesn't stop. It doesn't. The doctors are as burned out as the nurses. There're no ebbs, just flows. It doesn't seem to stop. My trailer shakes all night from the helicopters bringing in new patients.*

She donated platelets every month. They always needed more platelets because they only stayed good for a week. Sometimes they needed more blood too. The more blood transfusions they could give, the longer they had to try and save the twenty-year-old on the table.

I looked away from the statue at that thought.

The good news, she had e-mailed, *is that improvements in gear mean that Kevlar vests are stopping most shrapnel and protecting vital organs. The bad news is that arms, legs, and faces are still exposed. So when a blast rips through a Humvee, there are more survivors but heinous injuries. In Iraq, it's all polytrauma, multiple areas of the body. Whereas in the States, there's generally one bad area you focus on. Here we get head wounds, limbs that need amputating, and horrible burns all on one person. Sometimes three surgeons are working on the same person at the same time. We can save them, whereas in any other war, we'd have lost them. But it still breaks my heart. They've kept their lives but at a terrible cost.*

Then, a few days later, she felt less bleak.

You wouldn't believe some of the shrapnel I've pulled out of people. They all want their shrapnel, she wrote. *More than their Purple Hearts, they want the shrapnel.*

I forced myself to change thoughts. *Be present in the moment.* I gazed up at *David* again, at the cool white almost bluish marble, at his serene face, and drew what comfort I could. He'd been around for hundreds of years and would be here for hundreds more, through wars, droughts, plagues, and all the other disasters life can bring.

Most people, I gradually noticed, didn't spend that much time looking at *David*. It seemed like all they wanted out of their trip was the ability to say to the folks back home that they saw *David*. I wondered if it was true about other great sites, works of art and historic buildings and cathedrals.

There were a few art students who were sketching *David*, and I wished that I knew how to draw because that would have been a wonderful excuse to stare at him for hours. Maybe I could switch my major. Instead of psychology, I could study art, or art history, and come to Florence for a semester abroad. The thought made me very happy.

After I caught up with the rest of the girls, we left the museum and found a small bar/café that served sandwiches. I ordered us cappuccinos to go with our sandwiches.

"*Quattro cappuccini,*" the man behind the bar sang out, and immediately began an elaborate, dancelike routine that involved grabbing saucers and placing them in front of me, spinning the small white cups and then placing them with a flourish under the machine, pressing the coffee grounds, rotating the base into place, and then frothing the milk while a thin stream of coffee poured out directly into each cup. Then, again with a lot of elbow motion and a graceful turn, he added the hot, frothed milk to the drink, and when he placed the cup in front of me, I saw he had made a heart out of the milk, the froth, and the darker coffee that had mixed in.

I clapped, and he gave a small bow as he placed a tiny little spoon beside each cup. I loved this about Italy. I loved how even the mundane, like making coffee, was turned into a work of art. It reminded me that there was beauty in the everyday; I just needed to keep an eye out for it.

We took our food to the small table outside and ate in the shade. The cappuccino was creamy and warm. I felt the jolt of caffeine and sugar revive me from the walk and the hours of standing at the Academy Gallery. How was it possible for the cappuccino to taste so good when he used shelf-stable milk that didn't need refrigeration?

A woman walked by, and for a second, something about her reminded me of my mother. Which reminded me I was supposed to check my e-mail.

"Crap," I said out loud, filled with stomach-dropping guilt. "I've got to find a computer."

Katie looked at me with a silent, worried glance as if she thought I would have another meltdown.

"I promised my mom," I said. "I promised to check my e-mail every day. It's the only way to stay in touch."

By the time I came back from asking the bartender where to find a computer café, the rest of them had finished their lunch. They came with me to the Internet store and bought computer time as well.

As I waited for my message screen to come up, I overheard Lola chatting.

"You know, my parents are kind of freaking out about this trip," she said to Madison. They both logged on to computers down the row from mine. "They wanted me to call them every day." Her disgust was obvious. "Like that was going to happen. But I guess the least I can do is send them an e-mail now and then.

"God, I hope I'm not like that when I'm a parent," she said.

I couldn't tell if Lola was making fun of me or not, but it didn't matter. Even if she wasn't mocking me and my promise to e-mail my mom every day, it was still an obnoxious thing for her to say. I glanced over at Katie. Her gaze was down, focused on her hands at the keyboard, but she wasn't typing. She didn't have a naggy mother to placate either. It infuriated me that Lola could be so insensitive. Didn't she know how lucky she was? Both her parents were safe, they were home.

"You know, Lola," I said before I could stop myself. "There's a reason I want to e-mail my mom every day. It's because she's in danger. Every day. This is what she e-mailed me today."

I saw Katie and Madison exchange loaded glances.

"'Last night I was fifty feet away from a direct hit,'" I read out loud, my voice louder than usual. "'A mortar round hit two trailers away. Amazingly, no one was damaged. It did hit a bike rack, though. My new bike is totaled.'"

"Holy shit, Arden," Madison said. "But your mom is a nurse, right?"

It was nasty to feel vindicated, but I did.

"That's why we try to stay in touch every day," I said, looking at Madison but directing my words to Lola, who wouldn't look at me. "The chances that anything will happen to her are slim. But it's lawless. There's utter chaos, and lots of people hate us and want us dead."

There was total silence after that. I inhaled and exhaled, trying to calm down. The keyboards clicked and tapped as the girls started typing. I felt Katie glance over at me, but I wouldn't look away from the screen.

There was no cause to get so upset. Except it brought home again that our lives, mine and my mom's, were so affected by the war, while for everyone else it was meaningless. Right after my mom was deployed, it was hard for me to see people going about their business as if there were no war. The only signs that anyone was even aware of its existence were the yellow ribbon decals on cars saying "Support Our Troops." But the only "support" those people gave was spending three bucks at the gas station to buy the damn decal. It was easy to "support" the war when it demanded nothing of you.

I didn't want to write a bad or sad message to my mother. But thinking about the injustice of it got my hands shaking. I glanced over at Lola: plump, self-satisfied, feeling so superior to her parents, who'd never been to Europe. She laughed at something on her screen and read it out loud to Madison and Katie.

I couldn't write to my mom about this, about how I wished she weren't in Iraq, how I wanted her to have a normal job like everyone else. It wasn't fair to make her feel any worse about it than she already did. I kept deleting curse words, which kept cropping up like red welts from some sort of nasty rash.

How're things on base? I'm so glad no one was hurt. Will things quiet down a bit, do you think?

I couldn't think of anything else to write that wouldn't tip her off that I was upset.

Florence is beautiful, I wrote. *But I miss you.*

Peter's e-mail, when I clicked it open, wasn't the humorous distraction I was hoping for.

I don't know which category your friend falls into, he wrote in reply to my remark about Madison's Francophile nature. I glanced at the date and saw he'd e-mailed this yesterday. *Sometimes we see what we want to see, especially if it's something we've imagined seeing for a while. When it's finally there, right before you, maybe you only see what you want to. It's why I kissed you that night, you know. I saw what I wanted to see, until you pointed out that I was fooling myself. I still don't know if I should have apologized for then or not.*

I froze, reading that e-mail. He'd addressed a taboo subject without any warning and it threw me off. I wanted to write, *Don't you dare apologize.* I wanted to write, *That was random. Why bring this up all of a sudden?* I wanted to ask, *Do you love me?* Instead, I wrote, *Hey, I'm in Florence now. Bet you can't think of anything bad to say about Italian food. Don't try to tell me they don't know how to cook good food because frankly, if it's not Italian food, it's crap!*

I hit SEND and cursed myself for being a fool.

14.

"Ice cream!" Madison grabbed my arm, breaking the awkward silence that had descended once we logged off. "Don't you just absolutely need gelato right now?"

I pretended to think about it.

"Oh, stop it," she scolded. "I might die right now, this very minute, if I don't have one."

It was hard to argue with that. Any time was a good time for gelato.

We left the Internet café and walked toward the banks of the Arno River, past tacked-up posters for chamber concerts in various churches, tours, and even a circus that was in town.

"Arden, you're okay?" Katie asked softly as we entered the cool *gelateria*.

"Yeah," I said, managing a light smile. "Just moody sometimes. Nothing ice cream won't fix."

Madison and Lola were already debating which flavors they wanted from among the small mountains of creamy, cold gelato. One-half of the display was full of fruit-based flavors—

tangerine, cantaloupe, strawberry, lemon, blackberry, sour apple, coconut; the varieties went on and on. The second half held the chocolate and cream-based flavors—pistachio, Nutella, chocolate chip, dark chocolate, caramel, crème brûlée; again, the choices were staggering.

Madison grabbed my hand in her excitement.

"How do you choose?" she whispered.

It turned out we could taste as many of the flavors as we wanted to before committing ourselves to a choice. I tasted two flavors before feeling too guilty to ask for more. A cup of gelato cost less than two dollars; it seemed wrong to taste more than a few flavors. Madison had no such qualms. She kept flirting with the gelato guy and asking for more. She must have gone through seventeen tiny, colorful plastic spoons, each with a dollop of gelato, as she decided which flavors she wanted to order.

We crossed the Ponte Vecchio, the old bridge, which was full of shops selling expensive gold jewelry, and continued to the other side of the city, enjoying our ice cream. Most of the tourists stopped exploring right around there, and the city quickly became much quieter and cleaner.

There was a small park, a neighborhood place you'd come to after school, off to our right. Without saying anything, Madison veered off and walked there. Lola and Katie exchanged looks, then followed her.

Madison sat down on one of the swings, and as there were three others sitting empty, we all joined her.

"You okay?" Katie asked her.

"Mm," Madison said, which didn't actually answer the question.

Lola started swinging and I followed suit. Before long, Katie and Madison were pumping their legs and we were like the pendulums of an insane clock. I could feel my hair streaming out behind me and I felt like I was flying. I pumped as hard as I could up, then leaned forward as I swung back, my hair plastered against my back. I went up, up, up and then down so hard my stomach dropped and the chain snapped taut.

"She soars through the air with the greatest of ease," I hollered. "She's the daring young girl on the flying trapeze!"

Lola shrieked with delight as she tried to catch up to my heights. Katie and Madison were swinging hard, shooting their legs up, then leaning forward.

"I'm king of the world!" Madison cried.

"No, I am!" Lola laughed as she passed Madison on the way up.

"When I was little," Katie said, grunting a little with effort, "I wanted to be the girl who went over the top bar."

I knew what she meant. To swing so hard you went vertical and came down the other side. I wondered if everyone had that wish.

We slowed down, still laughing. I couldn't remember the last time I went swinging; it had been at least five years, maybe more.

"Good call," I said to Madison. "That was fun."

Her smile was lovely and I felt the urge to hug her, though I didn't.

I was leading the way to the Pitti Palace, one of the Medici residences during the height of their power in Florence, when I heard the sound of an explosion.

My heart, for a moment, stopped.

"Oh my God," I said, choking back a wave of panic. "That was an explosion."

None of the girls had even noticed the sound.

"What?" Katie said. "What are you talking about?"

For a second, I wondered if I'd imagined it. Was I having auditory hallucinations? But I knew I wasn't.

"That boom," I said, feeling shaky. "That was some kind of explosion."

"No, it wasn't."

"Yes," I said. "Trust me."

In Heidelberg, we lived near the front entrance of the post, and every afternoon at five-thirty, they fired cannons to mark the end of the day. I knew what a small explosion sounded like.

No one around us seemed perturbed, and I didn't hear sirens wailing in the distance. But the day suddenly felt ominous and cold. It hadn't been that loud and I hadn't felt any vibrations, which meant that it was either a very small explosion or that it was fairly far away. It didn't sound like it came from the old part of downtown across the river, packed with the famous and historic sites of Florence. Packed with the sort of targets terrorists would attack.

I thought of my mother and the terrible irony of my being at the site of a terrorist bombing traveling in Europe while she was in Iraq.

This explosion had sounded like it came from in front of us, the newer part of the city with hardly any tourists at all.

"Come on," I said, pitching my empty ice cream cup into an overflowing trash can. "Let's find out what happened."

Madison looked at me, bit her lip, and nodded. "Okay, but I don't want to see any dead bodies."

We'd been walking aimlessly for about ten minutes, trying to see if people were rushing anywhere, when we heard it again.

"See!" I exclaimed, my heart racing once more. "You see? Another one. What is going on?"

It seemed we were a bit closer to the source of the noise, but again, no one around us seemed the least bit concerned.

"I don't understand it."

"Maybe it's a construction site?" Lola suggested. She'd been quiet since we started our hunt.

"Maybe." It all seemed very odd and not a little suspicious. I was scared and wished that I spoke better Italian.

We'd come to a residential part of the city; the buildings were a bit shorter, newer, and easier to see around.

The third time we heard the same explosion, something caught the corner of my eye. I whirled to look at it, and in the space of a narrow alley, I saw a person, wearing silver, flying through the air.

"Did you see that?" I asked Katie.

She grinned. "I did."

And then she pointed to a flyer that we'd seen posted all over the city without paying much attention.

The circus was in town.

And they were practicing.

I started laughing. I had to lean up against the wall. Lola was already on the ground, howling.

"Terrorists," she gasped.

"Dead bodies!" I wheezed.

I laughed so hard my stomach hurt, my eyes watered, and I almost wet myself. I couldn't catch my breath. I howled with delight, and Madison's high-pitched hysterics just fed our laughter.

"Oh my God," Lola said when we could finally speak again. "That was priceless."

I felt deliciously weak and boneless from the laughter, the relief, and the sudden feeling that Florence was enchanted and nothing bad could ever happen to me here.

That night, at the convent, I woke up after a few hours of sleep, shifting until I found a comfortable spot. Lola lay sprawled on her back, snoring. I curled on my side, feeling the cool wall against my back and soaking in the feeling of perfect contentment. A feeling of well-being had stayed with me throughout the day, and now at night, I still felt wisps of it here and there. I wallowed in it. If I were I cat, I would purr.

"I love you, Dad," I whispered. Then I closed my eyes and fell asleep again.

15.

The next day, our meanderings brought us to the Piazza della Signoria, famous for its life-size replications of famous statues. The original *David* used to stand there before the powers that be decided he was too valuable (or vulnerable) to stand outside in the sun and the rain and the bird crap. Now there was a larger-than-life copy towering over the square, trying to make up in sheer size what it lacked in originality. There were other statues, classical Greeks and Romans, legends and myths come to life: a muscular man wrestling with a giant serpent, another kidnapping a naked, struggling woman. The intensity of emotion didn't fit with the laid-back, business-as-usual atmosphere of the square. It lent it an air of menace.

We sat down at the edge of the Neptune Fountain; Lola and Katie had left to buy cold drinks because between the hot day and the endless walking, Madison felt sick.

"I really don't feel well; I hope they come back soon," Madison said. She dipped her hands in the lukewarm fountain water and sighed.

"You're probably just dehydrated," I said. Every time Madison complained about feeling sick, Lola and Katie exchanged looks. It drove me nuts. This time was no exception. As soon as she said she felt sick and wanted a drink, the two of them shot up like well-trained retrievers and rushed out to find a vendor.

She did look sick. She was pale, with beads of sweat dotting her brow and upper lip. But I didn't understand the conspiracy to keep her secret malady from me.

"Have you guessed yet?" she asked, as if reading my thoughts.

"I think so." Because what could I say, You're driving me crazy with suspense?

"I'm pregnant."

That wasn't, actually, what I was thinking. But now wasn't the time to mention I thought she might have a thyroid problem.

"Oh, Madison," I said. "I'm so sorry." That didn't seem like the right thing to say. "Not that it's a bad thing, necessarily," I fumbled. "It's just that . . . you know . . . a surprise."

Madison looked like she weighed about a hundred and five pounds. She had a Hello Kitty shirt on with tiny pink bows on the sleeves and she'd scrawled on her tennis shoes in thick black marker. I realized none of this would necessarily affect an egg's ability to be fertilized, but she seemed so young it was incongruous to think of her as a parent.

"No," she said. "It is kind of a disaster."

"But you have a serious boyfriend?" I asked awkwardly.

"Ex-boyfriend, Rob. Who doesn't know. We broke up nine weeks ago. This"—she patted her flat belly—"is a little souvenir of our goodbye." She gave a watery chuckle, which was when I realized she was crying.

"I don't know what do, Arden. Katie thinks I should keep the baby, Lola thinks I shouldn't. And I agree with both of them."

I touched her leg. It was thin and felt fragile under my hand.

"Adoption?" I asked. I tried to think what I would feel, what I would do in her situation, but I couldn't wrap my mind around it.

"No." She shook her head. "I don't want to be pregnant. I wish it had never happened, but it did and I don't know what to do. Every choice I have is a bad one."

We watched people strolling by for a moment. I was both glad and sorry that she'd told me. Sometimes it was nice to think that other people didn't have serious problems in life.

"This trip was supposed to get me away from Texas and give me some perspective," she said. "It was all very impulsive. I wasn't planning to come, originally. But Katie found this great last-minute fare the week before she and Lola were leaving, and it seemed like a great idea once I found out I was preggo. I guess in the back of my mind, I was thinking that if I do have the baby, then I won't get the chance to travel and be silly with friends again." Her voice cracked.

"I think you could be a great mom, if that's what you wanted to do," I said. That's what I would want to hear if I were pregnant. "My mom was twenty-one when she had me. It's probably why we're so close."

"Really?"

"Yeah," I said, bumping her with my shoulder. "Really."

I saw Lola and Katie coming toward us and Madison wiped her tears.

"Nobody knows about this other than Katie and Lola and

now you. My parents don't know, Rob doesn't know. I haven't even been to a doctor. I guess the more people I tell, the more real it gets."

"Here you go," Katie said, handing Madison a chilled can of Fanta. "This'll help settle your stomach."

"Arden knows," Madison said, popping the tab and taking a sip. "I told her."

"Good," Katie said.

"It's about time," Lola said at the same time.

I realized then that it wasn't their secret to tell me and that they'd been waiting for Madison to tell me herself. In the midst of feeling very sorry for Madison, I felt a warm glow of friendship fill me.

While we waited for Madison to feel better, we shared a bag of roasted almonds Katie bought, watched the people strolling by, and played my favorite guessing game.

"The way the game works," I explained, "is that you guess where people are from based only on their clothes, shoes, glasses, and haircuts. If you can hear them talking, then it doesn't count." It was something I always did in the airport or when traveling.

"What kind of game is that?" Lola asked. "Everyone pretty much looks the same."

"That's not true," I said. "That blond couple with the crazy bright blue and red eyeglass frames? They're Dutch. The Dutch love funky eyewear."

Katie had her eye on a swarthy couple with a young child in a back carrier when someone shouted out Lola's name.

We all looked around and two guys walked up to us.

"Oh my God! I can't believe it." Lola jumped up and

hugged first one, then the other. "What are you doing here? I didn't know you were in Italy!"

I stood up when she leapt and watched them, hands in my pockets. Katie and Madison knew the two guys and everyone hugged each other.

"God, I can't believe it," Madison kept saying. "What are the chances of meeting someone you know in Italy? I mean really? That's so cool."

"Arden." Katie turned to me. "These are friends of ours from UT. That's Dean and that's John."

"Hi," I said.

"Arden goes to Vanderbilt. We met her on the flight over here," Katie said, as if that explained something. And maybe it did because they nodded.

"Hey," Dean said. John nodded shyly.

Dean had that indulged frat-boy look. His hair was straight and a little long, falling into his eyes right after he brushed it out of the way. He wore a wrinkled button-down shirt untucked over his khaki shorts. John was much shorter and had the beginnings of a beer belly, and his curly hair was already receding, making his forehead look really large. He wore a collared shirt tucked in over his belly and cheap plastic flip-flops. They seemed like an odd pair.

They joined us on the fountain.

"So what are you guys doing here?" Lola asked. She sounded breathless and giddy and kept touching her hair.

"I just finished a six-week program," John said. "Dean came to meet me and we're backpacking for a week."

"Art history," Dean said, leaning toward me. "Is he a faggot or what?"

He was too close to my face and I leaned back a bit. "Why?"

"What kind of guy studies art?" Dean asked, punching John on the shoulder. Though it was obvious he was used to this, John turned bright red. Lola laughed, but it wasn't her regular larger-than-life laugh. This one sounded fake.

"I don't know," I said. "What do you study?"

"Psychology. You know, all the shit that goes on in people's heads." Lola laughed again.

At school we called a psych major the major of lost souls. If you didn't have a plan, didn't know what else to do, you ended up in psych. It was true for me, but Dean didn't seem like the curious and outgoing psych student I was used to.

"Right. Talking about your feelings," I said. "That's pretty manly." I was like a dog trying to scare intruders off my territory. *Go away*, I thought, *just go away*. I couldn't explain my sudden, intense dislike of them. But in an instant I saw Lola change before my eyes from funny and easygoing to vapid and shallow. I had a bad feeling.

Dean mumbled something under his breath that sounded a lot like "bitch" while John stifled a laugh.

"So," Katie dived in. "How did you like the program? I've heard great things about it."

But John didn't want to talk about it and mumbled something that sounded like "it was good" or maybe "there was a lot of wood." I couldn't understand for sure.

Madison and Katie moved to sit between Dean and Lola as if they shouldn't have a clear view of one another. Lola ignored their efforts and moved so that she stood in front of them, leaving John and me to try and talk about the weather.

The guys had been hanging out with us for only a few minutes and already the dynamics between the four of us had changed.

Dean and John hadn't eaten dinner yet and wanted the rest of us to join them while they ate. We found a smoky little place and grabbed a table in the back. I don't know how much time had passed, long enough for Dean to have five or six beers, when Madison happened to see John's watch.

"You guys!" she yelled too loudly. "The time!"

"It's almost eleven," I said, looking at my own watch. "Why?" And then it sank in.

"Shit!" I grabbed Lola's arm.

"What?" She was very buzzed and couldn't understand what the problem was.

"We've got to get back before eleven or they won't let us in."

Katie jumped up. We all dug into our wallets, tossed some bills on the table, and rushed outside.

"Where do we meet tomorrow?" Dean asked.

I didn't get a chance to make eye contact with Katie and see if we could make up an excuse: a group tour of St. Francis's basilica in Assisi, a meeting with the pope in Rome.

"How about the fountain, where we sat?" Lola said. "Say, ten?"

"Great."

We couldn't wait any longer. We took off, running as fast as our wobbly legs could go.

We made it, but just barely. The nun, the same one who was always there, let us in and didn't seem pleased with us at all. I felt sick from my two beers and running. My heart was beating too fast and the room was spinning around me.

I collapsed on my bed.

"Oh my God," I moaned. "I think I'm going to be sick."

"Here, drink some water." Lola handed me her bottle and I drank. "Now just breathe for a moment; it'll pass."

I kicked my shoes off and stretched out, fully clothed. I heard Lola undress and put on her pajamas, which was a good idea, but at the moment it seemed a bit beyond my capabilities.

"You go to school with them?" I said after a moment.

"Yeah."

"Funny that you ran into them like that."

"Isn't it crazy?"

I was both sleepy and drunk, and it felt wonderful to lie in the dark room and not have to do anything. I was trying to think how to say that we shouldn't travel with them, that we should just keep it to the four of us girls.

"Dean was the first person I slept with," Lola said before I could figure out a diplomatic, persuasive argument.

"What?"

"It was during Christmas break and I was waitressing. He showed up one night. He bought a drink and we talked and he left me a huge tip. Afterward I went to his place and we slept together."

"Just like that?"

"I wanted to get it over with, you know? It's such a freaking burden, your first time. It seems like after a while, it counts for too much, so I wanted to get it out of the way. I'm nineteen. I figured, screw it." She giggled at the pun.

"Yeah, but . . . but . . ."

"I knew him pretty well from school; it wasn't like I'd picked up a stranger."

"But . . . ," I said, stuck like a broken record. "I don't— I mean . . . Why? Why him?"

"Because he's so good-looking and I knew him from school

129

and a lot of girls liked him. It seemed like a good idea. And it was, if you want to know."

"Oh."

"By the time school started up again, I ended it. We stayed friends because that's the sort of thing it was. Just casual and there were no hurt feelings."

Maybe this was normal. I wasn't sure. But it creeped me out a little. It made sex seem cold and calculating, something to get over with. I never thought of it that way. I wondered why they really broke up.

I wanted to ask more. To understand what and why and how she felt about it now. "Do Katie and Madison know?" I whispered.

She didn't answer and I realized that she'd fallen asleep. Pretty soon the sounds of her soft snores came at regular intervals, like waves on the shore.

I rolled on my side, tucked my hands under the pillow.

The closest I ever came to having sex was six months after my father died, on Peter Meyer's graduation night. In the end, it wasn't even close, but the thought of what could have happened that night, if only I was willing, haunted me for months. The memory of it still had the power to make me squirm under the covers.

After the graduation ceremony, the hugs and teary-eyed trips down memory lane, I'd somehow been pulled and dragged along to a party at someone's house. I didn't even know whose house it was. Everyone was there, drinking bottles of German beer out in the open since it was legal at sixteen to drink beer off post in Germany. A lot of people were moaning about the irony that when they went off to college, they wouldn't be able to (legally) do the things they'd done in high school.

I sat, wedged against the arm of an overstuffed sofa, leaning away from two seniors making out, wondering if I could find a phone and ask my mom to pick me up. I'd come without a car, and I didn't think my ride would be ready to leave anytime soon.

When I saw Peter's head, inches above everyone else's in the room, I expected to see a girl or two snuggled up against his side, but he was alone. I abandoned my little nest next to the making-out couple, who promptly sprawled out, taking over the vacated space.

"Hey," I said, walking up to him. "Congratulations."

"Arden," he said, blinking at me in surprise. "I didn't know you were here." His eyes seemed slightly unfocused, and I wondered how much he had had to drink. He was usually strict about drinking, not wanting it to interfere with his swimming and, God forbid, jeopardize his scholarship. But I guess he made graduation night an exception. I was about to say something when someone bumped me hard enough to make me stumble and spill some of my drink on the beige carpet.

"Let's get out of here before you get stepped on," he said.

He put a hand on my shoulder and steered me out the door into the next room. We were in an empty bedroom. His hand was large and warm and I tried not to want more.

"You're all knotted," he said. He set down his beer on a nearby console and put his other hand on my shoulder so that both hands rested on either side of my neck, and I shivered. "You need to relax, kid," he said, and pressed lightly, his fingers finding sore, achy points, raising goose bumps everywhere.

A part of me couldn't believe this was happening. I was getting a back rub from Peter Meyer on his graduation night. The other part was desperately trying to commit every detail to memory and also think of something to say that wouldn't sound moronic.

"You're good at this," I said. "If the swimming thing doesn't work"—I stifled a groan as he found and leaned into a knot—"you could open a spa."

"We do this to each other on the bus ride back from meets," he said, making me suddenly regret that I hadn't joined the swim team when I had the chance.

"Nice."

I could almost feel his shrug behind me. The noise of people in the other rooms was muffled here. It occurred to me that if any other two people were in here, they'd be on the bed instead of standing next to it. As soon as I thought that, I could feel myself blush and my shoulder tense, ruining all of Peter's work. As if reading my thoughts, he patted my shoulders and dropped his hands.

"So, Arden, what's your big plan?" He stepped away from me and sat down on the edge of the bed so we faced each other. My shoulders were warm from his hands, my hands tingled with the desire to touch him.

"What do you mean?"

"You've got college applications coming up soon; where do you want to go?" I tried to focus on our conversation, on words. Tried to get the thought of what it would feel like to touch him, to kiss him, out of my head.

"I don't know," I said truthfully. "I hadn't given it much thought." I'd had other things on my mind.

"I can see you in the South," he said, closing one eye and holding a thumb out like a painter getting ready to paint. "In a private liberal arts school, not too big, not too small. Say twenty-five hundred students. I'd say you'd be a good fit at William and Mary. Maybe Vanderbilt. You've got good grades, right?"

"It's graduation night," I said, dodging this bizarre line of questioning. "Why in the world do you want to know about my grades?"

"I'm just thinking I'm going to be in California and that's far away from everyone." He picked up my hand and looked at it. First at the back and then he flipped it and studied my palm, as if reading the lines.

"So why do you want me to go to the South?" I tried to concentrate on sounding calm, on keeping my breath steady and not gasping at the feel of his finger softly tracing the lines of my palm.

"I'd love it if you were in California with me, but I'm not sure it's the best thing for you."

Was he pulling my leg? He hardly knew who I was; how in the world had we come to talk about his thoughts about the best place for me? I wondered if someone had spiked my drink.

"Peter," I said, laying a hand on his hard shoulder. "I'll be fine, and you'll be great. They're going to love you at Stanford."

He smiled at me so sweetly that I leaned forward until our heads gently bumped together. The whole scene was so surreal that my heart wasn't even racing. His hand came up and cupped my face, and it was the most natural thing in the world to tilt my head and kiss him.

His lips were soft and dry. He spread his knees so I could step between his legs, and his arms went around me. It was an amazing kiss, better than anything I'd imagined, a perfect first kiss. I felt myself grow warm, my heartbeat picking up, and I ran my fingers through his hair, feeling the soft curls slip through. Then he leaned back, taking me with him, and we lay on the bed, facing each other, still kissing.

He brought his hand up to my hair. I felt my hair clip suddenly release and my hair tumbled free. His fingers tangled in my curls and he tilted my face up, deepening the kiss.

It felt wonderful to kiss him, to touch his shoulders and face, which was soft with a hint of stubble under the skin.

He wrapped one long leg around both of my legs, tucking me into the curve of his body, and I fit perfectly. We fit like two nesting spoons, matching up chest to chest, belly to belly, hips to hips. Without meaning to, my hands slipped from his face, to his chest, to his stomach, where I could feel ripples of muscles moving under my hands.

Peter's hand echoed mine and his long fingers skimmed along my ribs, coming to rest on my waist, his fingers on my hip bone near the waist on my jeans.

He whispered my name. I wondered what he was thinking, why he was kissing me.

"Stop," I said, putting a hand between our mouths.

"What?" he said, his voice husky. "What's wrong?"

What's wrong? I wanted to laugh. Everything was wrong. The guy I'd had a crush on for nearly a year was kissing me on graduation night and all I could think about was that he pitied me.

"No." I pushed his leg off mine, his hand off my waist, and rolled away from him. I sat up. My hair was tumbled and tangled and I pushed it away from my face. "No," I said again, shaking my head. "I'm sorry. I can't do this."

"Arden," he said, reaching out and touching my hair.

"It's okay," I said. I stood and brushed at my shirt as if I had crumbs all over me. "It's just not a good idea, yeah?" I shoved my hands in my pockets so he couldn't see that they were shaking. My whole body was shaking lightly, like a struck tuning fork vibrating, producing some inaudible frequency. Somewhere nearby, I was certain, dogs were howling to their owners' confusion.

"Okay," he said very gently. I wondered if I'd hurt his feelings. But this was Peter, our champion, the coolest senior in the history of the school. How could I hurt his feelings?

We walked out of the bedroom and back to the party.

"Arden—" he said, the loud music almost drowning him out.

But I didn't stop. I pretended I never heard him and he didn't try to stop me.

He left for Stanford a month later to begin training with the team.

16.

The next morning, we had breakfast at the convent, and neither Lola nor I brought up the conversation from the night before. We were all a little groggy from the drinking and not up for much chatting. I buried my nose in my coffee and tried to wake up.

"What do you want to do today?" I finally asked. Katie and Madison had already eaten their breakfast and were currently in the bathroom, showering and getting ready.

Lola shrugged. "Don't know. Depends on the guys, don't you think?"

"Right." I'd forgotten we'd agreed to meet them.

By the time we finished breakfast, showered, and dressed, it was almost ten and time to meet the guys.

We found them sulking at an outdoor café within sight of the fountain. They waved us over, and before we had a chance to sit down, Dean started complaining.

"The damn hostel won't let us stay another night," he said, then belched softly into his fist.

"So where's your stuff?" I asked.

"Left it in a locker in the train station for now," John said unhappily. "We can't find anyplace for tonight. Might have to sleep on a bench in the park. That or we move to Rome ahead of schedule."

"That's terrible." I was feeling sympathetic after my various fiascos with hotels this trip. Plus, from the looks of things, John had had to put up with Dean, who had been in a foul mood all morning.

John shrugged. "It's not like we were staying at the Ritz-Carlton to begin with. It was a pretty crappy place. The walls were full of bloody, smashed mosquito carcasses."

"I'd suggest our place," I said. "But it's for women only."

John shrugged again. "We'll figure out something in the end. We usually do."

We walked to the Duomo from the piazza, and the sun baked my arms and shoulders. I'd put on sunscreen that morning, but I could feel my shoulders and nose start to burn despite it. I looked over at Lola's olive skin with envy. She'd snorted this morning when I offered her a squirt of SPF 30.

"I don't burn," she said with a hint of disdain for the pale, weak-skinned of the world.

But Lola was covered in a fine sheen of sweat and didn't seem to enjoy the sun any more than I did. She kept glancing at Dean and fanning herself with one of the free maps she'd taken from the table by the door at the convent.

As we reached the Duomo, I was again blown away by its ridiculously impossible massiveness. In daylight it became clear how grimy it was from years of car exhaust and other pollutants. The gray overcast to the marble, however, only made the structure more imposing. It looked ancient and craggy and slightly foreboding.

We went inside and I sighed with relief at the cool, wax-scented air. It was dark inside after the bright glare of the midday sun and it took my eyes a moment to adjust. I was surprised by how much empty space there was. Except for the front quarter, the entire cathedral was as empty inside as a gigantic ballroom.

Tour groups followed their leaders through the empty shell of the cathedral like small herds of sheep. They were international sheep, to be sure, but they all looked alike in their lost, slightly anxious, pinched expressions.

I could smell myself, a mix of melted sunscreen, sweat, and my shampoo. I turned away from Katie and Lola and wiped my forehead with the tail of my shirt. Dean whistled quietly when my stomach was exposed. I dropped my shirt and glared at him.

Dean wanted to light a candle, but he wasn't Catholic and John talked him out of it.

"I'll light a candle for you, Dean," Lola said. "Someone needs to pray for you."

"Oh yeah, baby," he said as if she'd said something provocative.

She walked over to the table full of flickering white candles, dropped a coin in the donation box and lit a candle, then crossed herself. We all watched her.

Madison leaned over and whispered something to Katie, who nodded, looking unhappy.

"We're going to separate them," Katie whispered to me. "He's not good for her."

Madison, on a mission, touched Lola on the arm and pointed to a small covelike sanctuary with several benches, and the two walked over there.

Katie joined Dean and John in front of a huge painting of a saint.

Since she seemed to have things under control, I meandered away from their constant bickering and Dean's crude mocking. I found a tour guide in the middle of a lecture in English, so I sat down two pews away and pretended to be studying a painting of Mary while eavesdropping on what he had to say.

"At first no one believed the architect, Brunelleschi, when he said he could build a dome. Legend says that when the committee in charge of the building asked Brunelleschi to show them how he planned to build such an impossible thing, he handed them an egg and said, 'If you can balance this egg and make it stay without rolling, then you will know how I plan to build the dome.'" The tour guide spoke English with a thick accent. "They tried, of course, but they could not do it. Finally they said, 'Show us.' Brunelleschi cracked the egg in half and placed one half on the table. 'We could have done that,' they said. 'Ah,'" and here the guide raised a finger in a dramatic gesture. "'But you didn't,' Brunelleschi said. 'I had to show you, just as I will show you how to build the dome.'"

His group clapped, and then everyone rose and followed him farther into the cathedral. People from the group glared at me when I tried to follow. Everyone in the group wore bright orange stickers on their shirts, so I couldn't blend in with them.

Katie tracked me down shortly after that.

"Come on. We're leaving."

She didn't have to say it was because of Dean. I could hear Dean guffawing as John tugged him away from some unsuspecting tourist and the two stumbled, bumping into a Japanese couple reading their guidebook. I wished he and John would go ahead and leave Florence so it could be the four of us again.

As soon as we stepped out of the cool church, the hot sun and hotter pavement wilted everyone's resolve, so we decided to have lunch. When we passed by a cash machine, I stopped to take out some money.

Dean and John went into the souvenir store that was next to the ATM and Katie stayed with me. I was glad that she did; it made me feel like maybe we really were friends and that it wasn't a figment of my lonely imagination or simply a product of traveling and not knowing anyone else.

A trickle of itchy sweat crawled down my back and I hurriedly dug through my purse to find my card so I could withdraw some cash and go into the air-conditioned store.

I entered the store in time to see John and Dean paying for their purchases.

"What'd you get?" Lola asked with a flirty little smile.

Dean showed us the dirty postcard he'd bought, which was full of marble breasts from different statues around the city. In big red letters, it said CIAO FROM ITALIA.

"How come you didn't get that one?" I pointed out the version with penises on it.

"I didn't want to copy John. He bought two of those."

"Ha-ha, aren't you clever," John said. As a comeback, it was a little weak, but poor John had gone bright red, and I smiled at him to show that Dean was a twit.

After lunch, we strolled to Piazza Michelangelo. It was still too hot to do much of anything, and by now many of the stores and restaurants had closed for their afternoon break. The city seemed empty and abandoned. It was us and the pigeons.

"What should we do?"

"Dunno."

"My feet hurt," Katie said.

"My back hurts," Madison echoed.

I wanted to go back to the convent for a nap. I was dehydrated but really wanted to avoid paying two euros for a tiny bottle of water. Lola and I had a large two-liter bottle in our room that I could hardly wait to get my hands on.

"What are you guys going to do about tonight?" Katie asked.

"We're going to party all night long, baby!!" John and Dean high-fived. "So what do you say, girlies? Are you coming?"

"I wish we could, but we're in a convent," I said. "We have a curfew."

"We have a curfew," Dean repeated in a high-pitched voice.

"Wait a minute," Lola said, suddenly animated. "We could, though."

"We'd be locked out all night," Katie said.

"Who cares? We're on vacation," Lola said, nudging Madison to agree. Madison hesitated, seeming torn.

"We need our sleep," I said firmly.

"I agree with Arden," Katie said. She looked beseechingly at Lola and Madison.

"Oh, look. Madison and Lola have two mommies," Dean mocked.

I stiffened at the insult.

"Fine, then," Lola said. "How about this—we sneak them into our room."

"Sweet!" Dean and John high-fived again.

"We'll do it." Lola turned to Katie, Madison, and me, her eyes blazing. She gripped my arm tightly, hard enough to leave a mark. "It'll be freaking awesome. Just come by at one," she said to them. "That'll be safe. Don't buzz or anything. We'll be at the door to meet you."

"Lola, you're fucking amazing," Dean said, and kissed her hard on the mouth. "It's a date."

Lola beamed. John looked at me uncomfortably.

"I don't like it," I said, beginning to understand what this was about. I looked over at Katie, my one ally, but she just chewed her lip and let things slide.

"Come on, Arden," Lola said. "Don't be a wimp."

I would have stood my ground except for the expression on Lola's face. She was always joking and ready to have fun. But now her eyes and the tilt of her mouth looked vulnerable, hopeful. I could see her so clearly that it hurt and I looked away.

I sighed unhappily but didn't say anything.

"All right, then," she said. "We've agreed."

Lola and Dean happily plotted further details and I slouched in my seat by the fountain.

When I checked my e-mail that afternoon, there was a message from Peter.

An entire race is decided in the tension at the start of a race, in that moment when I'm crouched in position and before the blast to start. It's a moment as long as eternity. I can feel my heartbeat, muscles bunched, ready to go. The water is hypnotic and clear. Sometimes I think that if the horn doesn't blow, we would all stay there, crouched forever, frozen in time.

I lost the time trial before I even hit the water. That's the agony. I knew from the start. It was one of those days and nothing I did changed the course. In that moment before the jump, I'd already lost.

My heart twisted as I read his e-mail. I'd forgotten he had the Olympic time trials. And he'd lost. I never thought there was anything Peter couldn't achieve.

It made it worse that my parents were there. They flew in from Germany just to see me get blown out of the water. How fucking perfect is that? My mother cried.

I thought of you after I lost. I knew I could tell you and you'd feel bad. But how much can I feel sorry for myself when the person I'm complaining to has survived so much worse? It's a sport. It's a game. I lost. Time to get over it.

He'd told me it was a long shot for him to make the U.S. Olympic team. That he'd have to swim his very best on a day when the best swimmers weren't at the top of their game. But I didn't believe him. I knew Peter. He was always self-deprecating. I hadn't realized he was telling the truth.

I winced to think of his parents there, his mother crying. That wouldn't help him. If I had been there, I wouldn't have cried. I would never have let him see how disappointed I was he didn't make the team. I'd have taken him out for a cheeseburger and a stupid movie.

I didn't know what to write. My heart was warmed that he thought of me. I didn't want to write *Better luck next time*. I didn't want to write about my misadventures in Italy. What I wanted to write was, *I love you no matter what your time is, no matter if you never win. I wish I could have been there.*

But I couldn't bring myself to write that, so I didn't write anything.

That night, Lola and I got ready for bed in silence. John and Dean were both coming to our room. I'm not sure how it worked out that way, except that Katie didn't want to be involved. I didn't either, but with Lola as my roommate, I didn't have much of a choice.

"I can't believe you're still upset about this," she said, closing her lotion bottle with a snap. "I don't understand why you're making such a fuss. It's totally harmless."

I didn't want to pick a fight. Instead, I set my alarm for one in the morning because Lola didn't have an alarm clock, and we both lay down in our beds.

"It'll be fun," she said, her voice muffled by the pillow. "You'll see—we'll be talking about it later as the funniest part of the trip."

I'd been tired all day, but of course, now that I was lying in bed, I couldn't fall asleep. Lola, who seemed to be able to fall asleep in a nanosecond, was already snoring.

When the time came, I didn't even need the alarm. I'd been looking at the clock every ten minutes. I shook Lola awake.

"It's time."

"What? Oh, all right." She sat up. "You go down and let them in," she said.

"No. No way." I was fed up with being pushed around. "This was your idea. You go down. I'm staying here. I'll keep the door open, but that's it."

"For God's sake," she said, suddenly intensely annoyed with me. "You can be such a baby sometimes." She stalked out of bed, flinging aside the covers.

A few seconds later, I could hear them coming up the stairs. They were making a racket. I could hear Dean's loud laughter and John saying something back. It sounded like they were stomping up the stairs, and with the acoustics it echoed up, magnifying the sound.

When they finally made it to the fourth floor, I realized what was wrong. They were both piss drunk and everything seemed completely hilarious to them.

"Arden!" Dean bellowed when he saw me.

Lola elbowed him and I hissed for him to be quiet.

"Right, right, sorry about that," he said in a mock whisper.

I glanced over my shoulder, but the hallway was still deserted.

"Come on, hurry up!"

He banged his pack against the doorframe, causing it to shudder, which he found very funny and he doubled up giggling. Lola pushed him in, then nudged John, who wasn't any better off, after him.

Lola and I looked at each other in complete agreement.

"You need to be quiet." She shushed at them. "We'll all get thrown out if we're caught."

Dean tried to school his face to show suitable concern and then nodded.

I felt a surge of relief when we closed the room door after them.

We paused there for a minute and stared at one another, at a loss. The floor was made of terrazzo and would be too uncomfortable to sleep on. Somehow in all the plotting, actual sleeping logistics hadn't occurred to me. Or them, apparently.

"We are not sleeping on the floor," Dean said.

"Fine," I said. "Lola and I will share one bed and you guys take the other."

"There's no way I'm sharing such a tiny bed with another guy," Dean said.

"For God's sake," Lola said. "Who will you share a tiny bed with then, you ingrate?"

"I'll share the bed with you." He grinned. "And John can sleep with little Arden."

"Over my dead body," I said.

"I'm just being practical here," Dean said.

"That's fine," Lola said lightly, breaking the tension. "That makes sense."

"John can have my blanket and a pillow for the floor," I said. "No offense, John, but there's no way in hell we're sleeping together."

"None taken," he said.

I stripped my bed and handed the linens to John, who made a little nest for himself on the floor. I crawled onto the bed and pressed myself into the wall, feeling exposed with no sheet or blanket over me. Lola turned the light off and the four of us settled down. Except, of course, that I couldn't fall asleep.

I wondered if my dad was watching over me now, what he thought of all this. I wondered if he was watching over my mom too or if he had to keep switching back and forth between us. Of the two of us, she needed him more.

Go to Mom, I thought. *Make sure she stays safe.*

Tears welled up and there was nothing I could do to stop them.

John, perhaps because of all the beer he'd had, quickly fell asleep and was soon snoring.

From the other side of the room came the unmistakable sounds of clothes rustling, muffled giggles, and the occasional whisper.

My face flamed red with embarrassment. The more I tried not to listen to what exactly was going on, the clearer everything sounded. I couldn't understand how Lola could do that considering that John and I were six feet away.

Then somewhere between trying to block the sounds, trying to fall asleep, trying to figure out why people were so strange, I realized that John wasn't sleeping anymore either. To the sound track of Dean and Lola making out, he gazed up at me from the floor with a soulful, hopeful look.

"No way," I said, grossed out. I pointed at the floor. "You stay down there. Stay."

He looked hurt but rolled over, pulling the covers over his head.

I lay in bed, fuming.

The alarm rang at quarter to five in the morning, waking me with a start. It didn't seem to affect anyone else in the room, and I had to step over John's limp body to get to the clock and shut it off.

I stood by the bed for a moment, utterly groggy and disoriented. I'd had about two hours of sleep.

"John." I nudged him with my toe. "John, wake up. You need to get up."

He was hard to rouse.

"Huh?" he finally said, and his breath nearly knocked me over.

"It's time for you to go," I hissed. "People will be up soon."

"Right," he said, and rolled over, closing his eyes.

"No," I said, this time not bothering to whisper. "You need to get up." I kicked him, though in my bare feet it didn't seem to affect him much.

"What?"

"Up! Up! Get up!" I was tired and sore from sleeping badly. It was my room, my bed; and John smelled awful, which irked me no end. He sat up and rubbed his face.

I walked over to Lola's bed and poked Dean on the shoulder. "Wake up," I said. "Wake up!"

It seemed like an eternity before he opened his eyes.

"What do you want?" he growled at me. "Go away."

"It's time for you to go. It's almost five and people will be up soon."

"Ten more minutes." He started to roll over.

"No," I said, feeling like a pathetic drill sergeant. "You need to get dressed and leave."

This whole time, Lola stayed asleep. She lay there breathing, and it made me so angry. How did I get stuck with shepherding them out of our room?

After a lot of back and forth and tugging of various body parts, I was able to get Dean out of bed and into his clothes. With ill grace, the two of them heaved their packs on and followed me out the door.

"What are we supposed to do now?" John whined. "It's the butt crack of dawn."

"Not my fault," I said. "You can't stay here."

Dean didn't say anything but glared at me with bloodshot eyes.

I tiptoed down the hall and opened the main door and watched them clomp out dejectedly.

I crept back to our room. Lola, damn her, was still sleeping.

Every bone in my body felt tired, and my eyes felt like they had sand stuck under the lids.

I crawled into bed, pulling up the blanket from the floor. Thanks to John, it smelled like cigarette smoke and sweat. This time, I fell asleep in seconds.

17.

When I finally woke up again, the room was bright and hot. I rolled over and fumbled at my travel alarm clock, surprised to see that it was almost ten in the morning.

"Good morning." Lola was sitting on her bed, her journal in her lap. "I saved you breakfast." She tossed me a napkin-covered roll.

I tried to catch it but missed. It landed on the bed, scattering crumbs.

"Thanks. What time did you get up?"

"Couple of hours ago. You were completely out, you didn't want to get up for breakfast, so I let you sleep. When I came back, you were still sleeping."

"I hardly slept last night."

"I know. Me either."

I managed not to roll my eyes. Instead, I picked up the roll and broke off a piece. More crumbs fell on the bed.

"Where are Katie and Madison?" I asked.

"They went to the market. They're going to buy some fruit

and cheese for lunch. We figure we'll go to the river and have a picnic. Doesn't that sound great?"

I tried to suppress the feeling that I'd been abandoned. That Katie and Madison didn't care about me, didn't like me, that they were having more fun without me than they ever did when I was around. I tried to ignore the sharp pain that implied that in the end, everyone always left me.

"Whatever," I said.

"What?"

"Nothing." I took another bite of the bread. Without any jam or butter, it was plain and stale.

"What in the world is your problem this morning?" Lola said, her cheery voice fading to annoyance.

"My problem?" I could feel my voice rise. "What's *my* problem? Last night is my problem. Or don't you remember?"

I wanted her to say she was sorry about last night. I wanted her to say something about what happened between her and Dean in her bed last night; why she would do that?

"Last night was crazy," she said, kind of laughing. "Wasn't it a blast?"

It was like she lit a fuse around gas fumes. I felt my temper explode in a sudden whoosh.

"You think I enjoyed myself last night?" Too many words wanted to come out at once. I took a deep breath and tried again. "It's disgusting to have sex in our room with two other people six feet away."

"What?" She almost shrieked. "I did not have sex!"

"Whatever. I could hear you."

"It wasn't what you think." She grabbed my arm, forcing me to look at her, and her hand was as cold as her eyes.

She was finally saying the things I wanted her to say. But it wasn't any good. She was lying, and it wasn't making me feel any better.

"Whatever." I held on to my righteous anger. "It was wrong to sneak them into a convent. I'm not even Catholic and I think it's wrong. What kind of person does that?" Her face had gone white. "And then to actually make out with him? I know you still have a crush on him, but I can't figure out why anyone would ever have sex with such a loser in the first place."

She dropped my arm. "I don't have to sit here and listen to this."

"No, you don't," I said, spurring her on. "You never have to do anything you don't want to, do you? It's everyone else that has to do what you want."

She grabbed her bag, put on her shoes, and left the room, slamming the door behind her.

The room was silent, but it still felt loud in the aftermath of the fight.

I rubbed my face, trying to get rid of the cold nervous sweat on my body and the adrenaline rush that left my hands a bit shaky. Why did I feel so betrayed? Lola was someone I'd met a week ago. I usually never let such new acquaintances upset me so badly.

I missed my mother. I was beyond tired, not just from not sleeping last night, but bone tired, soul tired. Tired of worrying about my mom all the damn time. Tired of missing my dad. Tired of what felt like an endless climb up a steep mountain. Would I ever get to the top and be able to rest?

For the past three years, I'd felt like a ball of grief and worry getting smacked around the court by other people's decisions. My father's misplaced faith in German traffic laws, my mother's deployment to Iraq, my mother's decision to sell the house, even

Lola's decision to let Dean and John spend the night. I was tired of being the ball. I wanted to be the one holding the racket.

I didn't want to sit around the convent and wait for Katie and Madison to come back. I didn't want to deal with Lola and her insecurities. God knew I had enough of my own. Suddenly it occurred to me that I didn't have to. Like Brunelleschi, I would crack my egg and show them my solution.

I found the lady who ran the convent.

"I want to pay," I told her in Italian. "I'm leaving."

I scrawled a quick note and slid it under Katie and Madison's door.

Have fun, guys, I wrote. *I had such a great time with you, but it's time for me to move on. I'll be at the house in Sardinia for the next two weeks or so if you feel like changing your plans.*

I wrote down the address and signed my name. I knew they wouldn't take me up on it. Sardinia wasn't on Katie's list of places to see. It wasn't even mentioned in her European guide-book. But this way, I didn't feel too rude about leaving.

With a burst of energy, I quickly gathered all my belongings and hurried down the dark stairwell.

I walked to the train station, heart beating a little fast, worried I would run into Katie and Madison before I arrived at the station. I didn't want another confrontation. I wanted to leave it all behind. I had joined them on an impulse, and it seemed right to leave them the same way.

I made it to the station safely and bought a ticket to Bologna. There was a major airport in Bologna where I could catch a short flight to the second-largest island in the Mediterranean. No more delays. No more distractions. It was time to go to Sardinia. There was a small house on the edge of a tall cliff waiting for me. It was time to stand at the edge and take a good look down.

18.

The train ride was only an hour. It was warm in the compartment and the rocking motion was soothing. I leaned my head against the window and watched the vineyards and farms and walled villages up on high hills come and go. The large window was cracked open, letting in enough breeze to keep the train car almost comfortable. I didn't let myself think about Lola or the night before; I didn't let myself wonder how Katie and Madison would feel when they came back to the convent and found all my things gone. It was surprisingly easy to keep my mind perfectly blank. When my stop came, I had to make myself stand and disembark. All I wanted to do was stay in my seat and keep riding forever.

I'd once read a set of speeches Admiral Stockdale had given to the Marine Corps Amphibious Warfare School. Admiral Stockdale was the highest-ranking POW in Vietnam. He'd been held captive for seven and a half years. He was tortured, kept in solitary confinement for four years, shackled in leg irons for two of them.

His lectures were about the moral codes he believed in, the thought process that helped him cope with his long, incredibly difficult imprisonment. He followed the code of the Stoic warrior, diffusing his fears and desires by taking stock of the things under his control. He let go of anything he couldn't control; he stopped craving it and focused only on the few things he was in charge of: his moral purpose, his emotions, his thoughts. Everything else: pain, loneliness, the opinions of others, material goods, he let them go. It was the key to happiness, he said. To sanity. To living a good life.

I often thought about Admiral Stockdale.

He suffered a lot during those seven and a half years. He went from commanding a thousand people to being a despised criminal. His leg was broken twice and healed badly. He limped for the rest of his life. Yet he described the trials and horrors and beatings in a matter-of-fact way. They were there; he endured them. But they did not touch his soul, his inner convictions of who he was, what his purpose was.

I read his lectures before my father died. My mother had returned from a conference where they handed out copies, and she recommended I read them. I was riveted by his account of his prison time, of his philosophy studies (he was a graduate student at Stanford) and how they helped him survive. John McCain had been in the same POW camp as Admiral Stockdale, and after reading that, I read McCain's book on personal courage. My father read the speeches as well, and for weeks afterward we all talked about the meaning of courage, of Stoicism and its indifference to the externals in your life.

After my father died, I compared my suffering to Stockdale's experiences. I thought how he would grieve but not be devastated by the loss if he were in my place. When my mom was deployed, I thought of him again. I knew he would be braver than I, stronger. I wanted to dismiss him, scoff at his teachings. How could I let go of my fear for my mom? How could I stop wanting my dad back with me? I didn't know how I could be "indifferent" to those things even though they were out of my control and I shouldn't crave them.

I thought, perhaps, I would relate better to a book by Stockdale's wife or his kids. They knew what it was like to sit and wait and worry. For seven and a half years, they wondered if he was alive or dead, if he was hurt and in pain. They wondered if they would ever see him again. In comparison, my mother's fourteen-month deployment and our regular e-mails were a cakewalk.

In the end, it was a question of self-pity. Sardinia was always our place, where we could be together, happy and safe. Now my dad was gone, my mom was in danger every day, and the house was about to be sold. How, Admiral Stockdale, how could I stop the longing?

19.

The last time I'd been to Sardinia was three years earlier. My mom took leave between leaving Texas and arriving in Germany, and we spent two weeks in Sardinia, a sort of welcome back to Europe.

When we arrived, no one had stayed in the house for over a year.

The houses on the mountain have large water tanks that supply the water for the houses. When my dad went to check on the level in the tank, he found the lock broken and the tank empty. We'd heard that people try to steal water, but this was the first time it had happened to us. Until the water truck came and refilled the tank, we'd have no water to wash with or flush the toilet. My dad tried to get the water truck to return to the house and fill the tank ahead of schedule, explaining in broken Italian that there was no water, *niente*, nada, zip. I climbed the stairs to my room and peered under the bed and in the closet to make sure there weren't any mice or snakes or anything else lurking there.

In the bathroom, I found a yellow stain in the sink from a steady drip, which had dried now that the tank was empty, a murky film of dust, dead flies, and something else: a live scorpion, trapped in the bathtub. It was black with a curving tail and a stinger on the end. I screamed for my parents to come up.

Without wasting any time, my dad left the water company on the phone, dangling in the kitchen, took one look at the scorpion, slipped off his shoe, and killed it.

He lifted his shoe and we both peered for a moment at the smashed, juicy remains.

"Eww!" I said, in delayed reaction. "Ew, I'm never getting in there!"

I did a scared-disgusted wiggle dance, hopping in place and brushing off invisible crawlies.

"Arden," my dad said, exasperated. "Calm down."

"Calm down?" I said. "There was a freaking scorpion in the shower! Not that it matters since there's no water to shower with in the first place."

"We'll have water by the end of the day," he said reasonably. "And a scorpion's bite is no worse than a bee sting."

"That's not true," I said. "They're deadly. Like a snake or a black widow."

"You need to stop watching so much television," he said, starting to lose patience.

Then he said something that I will never forget.

"Sweetheart," he said. "You won't always have us around. You have to be able to take care of yourself and do what needs to be done." He paused and looked at me. Really looked at me. He might have put his hand on my shoulder or maybe not. I can't remember, but I can feel it, a warm weight, a steady presence calming my invisible itches. "It's not always pleasant to do necessary things. But part of being an adult, of being independent, means that you see what needs to be done and you do it. No muss, no fuss. Right?"

Reluctantly, I nodded.

At the time, it was just another talk. I'd gotten more and more of them as high school dragged on. Self-sufficiency, self-reliance, big ideas about what makes a person strong and steady.

He was right: by the late afternoon, a slow, lumbering truck came and filled our water tank. We put on a new lock, better and stronger, and with only that slight delay, we started on our vacation. That one scorpion was the only one we found in the house, and no one was bitten or otherwise assaulted.

In some ways, I'm lucky that little talk stuck in my mind. It could so easily have slipped into the vague mass of hazily remembered events like his pep talks after I lost an important soccer game, after I lost the election for vice president in ninth grade. I know he must have said something nice when I left for my first homecoming dance, all dressed up in a ball gown and a corsage on my wrist. He certainly took a lot of pictures. But I don't remember his words.

I was grateful that I remembered something useful. I wished it weren't so relevant.

The rest of that vacation was uneventful. We went out to dinner, we relaxed at the beach. I went off by myself a lot. I could always find people to hang out with. Shyness in Sardinia was never a problem for me.

Everyone wore bikinis, even the older ladies, and I worried that my tummy pudge looked awful. I envied the slim, olive-skinned girls who wore pale pink bikinis and looked like they wouldn't know cellulite if it sat on their faces. I usually wore board shorts over my bikini bottom and hoped they'd think it was an American fashion statement.

That's what I remember from my last vacation with my dad.

Worrying about my figure and freaking out about a dead scorpion.

The plane to Sardinia was small and rickety. My seat had frayed upholstery, and the takeoff and landing were ridiculously steep and bumpy. The thin woman sitting next to me was terrified during the entire flight. I know this because she looked straight ahead, and knuckles white as her hands gripped the seat rest. Apparently, she was gastrointestinally sensitive to fear, and with each bump, each unidentified noise reverberating from the wings or under our feet, she passed gas.

I didn't know which would kill me first, the plane ride or the noxious fumes, but I hoped one of them would do it quickly and end my misery. After a while, forsaking all subtlety, I leaned as far as I could away from her and pulled my T-shirt over my nose. I pressed my forehead against the plastic window and gazed at the land and, later, ocean below me.

Everything looked so small and placid from above. But I knew it was more spectacular from the ground. You lost the details that make the countryside seem alive, that make the ocean seem like it could wash away any stress, any problems you might have.

We landed with three hard bumps that scared a grand finale of farts out of my seatmate. When we were allowed to unbuckle and disembark, she stood and grabbed her leather handbag without making eye contact with me.

I found my pack on the luggage carousel and went to find a

taxi to take me to the cottage. The taxi driver was a man in his fifties with a scraggly unshaved face full of white stubble. He smoked the entire ride and spoke in a rough dialect I hardly understood, so I didn't bother making conversation. I unrolled the window and spent the ride feeling the warm wind blow on my face and watching the dusty green shrubs and beige rock formations fly by. As he went around each blind curve on the narrow lane, he tapped his horn a couple of times. The road wasn't really wide enough for two cars, so in the daytime cars honked their horns as they came around the curves; at night they flashed their headlights. The comfort of this familiar insanity made me smile despite myself.

Every once in a while I caught a glimpse of the ocean, its blue brighter and deeper than the cloudless sky above, stretching out as far as I could see before it disappeared as we drove around a bend.

When he pulled up in front of the house, I wasn't ready.

I'd been daydreaming. The hot sun, the warm wind, the hypnotic flow of the scenery flashing by, requiring nothing of me, had lulled me into letting my guard down. I had my eyes half closed, basking in the warmth. When the taxi slowed down, I looked around, expecting a traffic light or a pedestrian crossing. I sat up and my heart beat fast when I recognized the houses on the street.

He stopped in front of the cottage, engine idling.

The house was smaller than I remembered and it brought on a weird sense of déjà vu. I'd been thinking about it for so long that to be here again in person was almost anticlimactic.

I roused myself and paid the driver. Then I hauled my pack and carried it to the kitchen door, which faced the street but was actually the back door of the house. I checked the water tank. I had ordered a service truck to come the week before. The lock was still on, the tank full. I pulled out the key from my purse and unlocked the door.

I had never before come to the house alone.

The kitchen was dark and smelled musty. I walked over to the window, drew back the curtain, and opened it to let the breeze blow in.

The house was clean because the real estate agent had arranged for a woman to clean it, but it felt unlived in. Houses can tell these things. I walked a circuit of the house, peering into my parents' bedroom, climbing the stairs to peek in the bathroom (no scorpions in the tub), and finally made it to my room. Not knowing what else to do, I unpacked, putting away my wrinkled T-shirts, beat-up shoes, underwear, and shorts in the hutch against the wall.

I was here and following my father's advice: I was doing what needed to be done. Sometimes, self-pity or not, that was the best you could do.

I padded downstairs in bare feet and tried to see the house from a stranger's point of view. To a stranger, none of the furniture in the house matched. Everything had been picked up over the years from stores or neighbors moving and leaving behind furniture we could use. Strangers wouldn't see the lazy mornings, the late-night dinners, the long talks about anything that struck us as interesting: the geology of the island, the mysterious history of the vanished Etruscans, my father's childhood in Florida and all the animals he'd had as pets. They'd see a scratched wooden table and mismatched chairs, a blue sofa with red swirls, years out of date, and a small white wicker bookshelf with paperbacks left behind, a few board games, and a small stereo with a radio and a stack of classical CDs.

Without really deciding to get started, I found myself eyeing various things, trying to decide what I would take back with me. That's what I was here for, after all. To strip the place like a car thief strips a car for its valuable parts.

There were several ceramic plates with the traditional turquoise, white, and black pattern that my mother had bought years ago. The plates were coming home with me, I decided.

But as much as I looked, I couldn't find anything that captured the spirit of the place. The whole was more than the sum of any of the parts. How could I take the breeze that came in and fluttered the curtains? How could I bring home the smell of the house that was probably a combination of Italian cleaning products and the dry air of the island but that evoked childhood vacation in my mind?

I rifled through the kitchen, finding a half-melted plastic ladle from the time I'd tried to make dinner and let it rest on a hot burner. The smell of burning plastic lingered in the house for days. That and the chipped mug my dad always had his coffee in joined the plates.

My meager pile, sitting on the kitchen counter, only served to echo how empty the house was without my parents. It was a house that deserved people. Maybe it wasn't such a bad thing to sell it. Coming here would never be the same again.

20.

I ended up leaving the task of finding memorabilia that were both tangible and portable for later. My pile of loot remained on the table, and I left the house to walk down to the bottom of the hill to the small rental agency a few blocks away.

I lied, telling them I'd driven a scooter before.

"It's been a little while, though, and it was in the States," I said. "The scooters are different here. Could you show me where the gas and brakes are on this model?" I was impressed with how confident I sounded and how straight-faced I bluffed. Lola and Madison, I knew, would be impressed.

I signed a lease agreement. I had a return flight to Bologna in two and a half weeks, and from there a flight to Frankfurt. I'd see our military friends in Mannheim and Heidelberg for a few days and then fly home to Nashville. End of trip. End of story.

I pushed the scooter out to the street and then, hoping they weren't watching me through the agency's front window, I turned it on and revved it a couple of times to make sure I had the correct handle for gas. Trying to look like I knew what I was doing, I straddled the bike and then carefully turned the handle for gas and drove away.

It took me a little while to learn the right balance, and I'm sure I looked a bit wobbly. I tended to twist the gas too strongly at first and jerk forward whenever I started going. I practiced around the quiet neighborhood near the cottage. It was late afternoon and people were coming back from the beach. Stopping was touch and go, and I used my feet more than I should've to keep from falling over, scooter and all. But in the end, it wasn't rocket science. I wasn't about to enroll in any motocross races, but I had the hang of it enough to drive to the beach and back. I hoped.

My first errand on the scooter was to the grocery store, filling the small cargo container with milk, eggs, cheese, and a paper bag full of purple-black cherries.

On my way back to the house, I passed by a funeral taking place at one of the smaller churches in town. There was one large church in the town, Renaissance-style with black-and-white marble. This was a two-story-tall church with heavy wooden doors, dark with age, tucked on a street with buildings on either side. The flowers caught my eye first and made me wonder if there was a wedding. Then I noticed the casket and thought, no, a funeral instead. I saw the mourners going into the church, dressed in black dresses and suits. At the top of the stairs, patiently waiting for them, was a small, dapper man in a dark gray suit and a small boutonniere. He had a tidy mustache and his hands were clasped together in front. *It doesn't get easier,* I thought, *and as bad as it hurts now, the funeral isn't the hard part.*

When I returned home, I made myself an omelet with

cheese and rosemary picked from the garden and brought it out to the back patio overlooking the cliff and the ocean.

The wind had picked up slightly, as it always did in the evening. I couldn't hear the ocean from this distance, I couldn't smell it, I could barely even see it in the fading light. But it was there and I was glad.

I waited until I could see stars. Until the moon, a crooked white smile that reflected on the distant waters, had risen.

Then I made myself get up and wash the dirty dishes.

I put on a CD of Bedřich Smetana's *The Moldau* and, to the sweeping sound of violins, climbed the stairs to my room. I didn't want to go to sleep in a quiet house. I wanted to pretend, if only for a while, that my parents were down there listening to the music, enjoying a glass of *digestivo*.

I lay down on my bed and placed my fingertips to the glass pane of the window. For a moment, I could almost swear I heard their murmurs. I fell asleep wishing that were true, knowing it wasn't.

In the morning, I walked down to the café and ordered a hot chocolate and pastry for breakfast. The proprietor, Roberto, recognized me and we spent a few minutes chatting.

Even after five days in Italy, my Italian was still rusty. I struggled to find the right verbs.

"*Sono in università,*" I said.

"*Bene,*" he said, as if impressed with my great acumen. "*E tua madre e tuo padre, dove sono?*" We paused for a moment while the steam hissed inside the metal pitcher as he heated the milk for my drink. He kept looking over my shoulder, as if expecting to see my parents coming in through the door behind me.

"*Mia madre è in Iraq.*"

He made a tsking sound and didn't charge me for the thick, creamy hot chocolate.

"Is bad, yes? Iraq?" he said in English.

"Yes," I said. "It's very bad."

Then he asked the question he was bound to ask.

"*Et tuo padre, dove sta?*"

"My father is gone," I said in English. I saw he didn't understand. I didn't know any of the euphemisms in Italian. Passed away. Lost his life. No longer with us.

"*Mio papà è morto.*" My dad is dead.

"*Davvero?*" he asked, shocked. "*È terribile!*"

"*Sì.*"

We were speaking of the very basics. My father is dead. That is terrible. But in a way, it was good to speak so clearly. No false words of comfort. No euphemisms for an awful fact but looking at it head-on and saying it like it was. And here was someone who knew him. In Nashville, no one had ever met my father. They might feel sorry for me when I told them that my father had passed away when I was sixteen, but they would never grieve for him. Sometimes it felt like no one but my mother and I ever knew he existed. All the moving we'd done over the years meant there wasn't a large crowd at the funeral. My grandmother and uncle and his family came. Some of their friends were there for support. A few neighbors and members of the congregation. But no one who really knew my father. With the exception of family members, there were a lot of dry eyes in the room.

Yet on an island in the Mediterranean, a café owner felt an awful shock at the two-and-a-half-year-old news of my father's death. He called out to his wife working the cash register and rapidly filled her in. Her face too slackened in shock for a moment, and then she rushed over to me and gave me a big hug, smelling of perfume.

"He is with God," she said in Italian. She clutched my hands tightly and stared into my eyes. "He is with God." She pointed with a short, plump finger to the ceiling.

They wanted to know what happened, how old he had been. I did my best with my limited vocabulary. The struggle to find the right words sheltered me from tearing up as I usually did when people started asking for details. In Italian, nothing sounded as bad. I'm sure my explanation was bungled and confusing because they both listened with furrowed brows and occasionally shared puzzled looks.

After a while, more customers came and they left to serve them. I took the opportunity to slip away.

Finding the town's only Internet café, I stopped the scooter in front of it. Several large fans with rotating heads were stationed throughout the small, un-air-conditioned room.

I logged on and began writing my mom.

I'm in Sardinia, Mom. I just came from the café and Roberto wouldn't let me pay for my drink. I told him about you and about Dad. As you can imagine, he and his wife were in shock about it. Funny to think how in their minds, he's been alive all this time.

The house is clean but tired-looking. I think the new owners will probably do a lot of renovating. Then, as if my fingers had a life of their own, I saw words appear on the screen. *I can't tell you how much I miss you. I wish you and Dad could be here. I can't fall asleep sometimes because my heart beats too fast, I'm so scared of a midnight call with bad news. I'm scared of the day I log on and there's no message from you.*

I'm tired all the time, I wrote. *I hate that you're over there. I hate that all I can do is count down days until you're back while at the same time knowing that date could change. I know that in the end, you're not safe anywhere. Not really. But being over there is so much worse.*

I didn't mean to tell you any of this. I don't want to make things any harder for you. But I know you pretty much guessed it anyway and I don't want to keep pretending.

I stopped for a moment, watching the cursor blink in front of me like a heartbeat. Basic facts. No false words of comfort. It was the truth and I felt like I had to tell it.

I know there's nothing either one of us can do about it. It's just about getting through it. I don't think I've told you that I'm so proud of what you're doing. You're saving lives and it doesn't get more important than that.

I love you, Mom. Please be safe. Love, Arden.

I hit SEND before I could change my mind. I had insisted my mother share with me her hardships. It was time I shared mine with hers.

Then, feeling like I was in the midst of an out-of-body experience, I found myself writing Peter.

I'm sorry again that things didn't work out like you'd hoped at the trials, I wrote. *It must be intense to keep coming to the same pool, to keep swimming those endless laps. I know you must relive the time trials and it must burn, knowing you weren't your best on the one day when it mattered.*

My hands started shaking a bit and were clumsy. I hit the wrong keys and had to go back and fix the words. My heart was beating faster and my mouth was dry.

I've relived that night so many times and I wish I could go back and change things. I have always regretted pushing you away on your graduation night. I don't want to ruin our friendship because it's very important to me. You are so important to me. I don't know how to say this . . . but—

But what? What could I tell him? That I loved him? That I wished he could be here now? That I thought he was beautiful and sexy and even if I could only have him for a night, I'd take him?

And what if he squirmed uncomfortably in his chair when he read my e-mail? What if my e-mails were a pleasant distraction to him, a way to keep in touch with folks from high school? For all I knew, he had dozens of army brat friends he kept in touch with.

I took a deep breath. Well, so be it. It was past time to lay down my cards and stop pretending. If that's how he felt, then it was time for me to find out.

I like you, I typed. *A lot. A lot more than I've ever let you know.*

I hit SEND and hoped for the best.

I drove to Cala Girgolu, my favorite beach with the rock formations. The sun felt intense, making shimmering waves on the pavement.

It had been thirty minutes since I'd sent the e-mails, and chances were neither my mom nor Peter had read them yet. It was as if I hadn't written anything. Except my words were out there, waiting in their binary forms for the right code to unlock and eyes to read them. I reminded myself again that it was done. No point worrying about something you can't change. Whoever said those wise words might as well have recommended not burning your finger when you touch a hot stove. Good advice but impossible to follow. Squaring my shoulders and tucking the towel under my arm, I made my way to the beach.

The beaches in Sardinia didn't stretch out for miles like the shores of Florida or Texas. The shoreline was rippled, so each beach was a small sandy cove flanked by large, smooth boulders, scraggly growth, and stunted trees. Most people stopped at the first cove or two, but I kept climbing over the rocks, picking my way through the undergrowth until I reached a cove that while not completely empty wasn't full of blankets, sunbathers, and splashing kids. I loved the large rocks that spilled into the water. One of my favorite things to do when I was young was sit on a rock in the water that was high enough to be dry. I'd splash my feet when I needed to cool them, then lie back and feel the rock's hot, knobby surface imprint on my skin.

I carefully spread out my towel and pulled off my dress. I hadn't been exercising for the past few weeks and I felt it now exposed in a bikini, no board shorts this time. But no one paid much attention to me, and I sat on my towel, legs sprawled in front of me, and watched the small waves rippling toward the shore.

I wished at that moment that I had someone with me. Someone I could turn to and say something stupid, like, "Isn't it so hot?" or, "Should we have seafood for dinner?" Katie, Lola, and Madison would love Sardinia, hanging out at the beach, riding on scooters. I hated that leaden feeling I got every time I thought of them, this vague sense of shame. They shouldn't be important enough in my life to matter. But our time together had ended badly, and it felt like my fault. Leaving them so abruptly had seemed like the right thing to do. It hurt to admit that I missed them. Were they pissed off at me? Had I hurt them? Maybe they wouldn't care.

Self-pity again. But Admiral Stockdale wasn't here either.

My high dive that had started when I got off in Paris had

me falling through France and Florence. I plunged past them until I reached the water in Sardinia. But now that I was here, I felt as if I had landed in an empty pool. That was what happened, I guess, when you never looked down.

The sharp sun hurt as it glinted and glanced off the water, so bright it felt like daggers in my eyes.

Two little girls played in the water in front of me. They built a sand castle, then giggled as they stomped it down. They had skinny arms and legs and big round tummies. Their hair was matted and tangled, and they screamed every time a wave crashed near them.

They noticed me watching them, so I smiled. They waved, then raced each other into the waves. It doesn't get much better than this, I wanted to tell them. Don't forget days like this when you're all grown up.

I was starting to burn, so I gathered my crumpled dress, my sandy towel, and trekked back to my scooter. I stuffed the towel in the compartment and, straddling the scooter, turned the ignition on.

It made a couple of coughing sounds, like an old man, and then fell silent. I tried again, heart beating faster, and again, I got a few weak coughs and a sputter. I stumbled off the scooter and stood there, arms dangling limply by my sides.

"Help me, please," I said out loud. "I don't know what to do."

I don't know what I expected. A sudden ray of light, like in a religious calendar? A chorus of angels singing hallelujah? Or perhaps manna that would float down like cotton candy from heaven to feed my body and soul? I don't even know who I was praying to, God, my dad, or myself?

Instead, I felt a hand on my shoulder and a voice by my ear ask, *"Ciao, bella, che succede?"*

I shrieked in surprise.

He stood there, a half grin on his face that faded as he caught sight of my splotchy, teary face. He wasn't much taller than me, with very dark skin and curly black hair.

"*Stai bene?*"

"No," I said, and kicked the tire. "This stupid thing won't start."

The stranger frowned thoughtfully and examined the scooter with the same gravity and delicacy as a doctor examining a patient with a mysterious illness. I saw him straighten with a jerk and I could swear he tried not to smile.

"What? What is it?"

"It's all right," he said in English, patting my shoulder awkwardly. "It's only out of petrol."

I stared at him for a moment, wide-eyed. "Are you joking?" I asked.

He shook his head.

I'd alternately been cursing the rental agency and myself. Now that the rental agency had been absolved, there was only myself to kick and laugh at. It never occurred to me that it hadn't come with a full tank.

"That's the dumbest thing I ever heard," I laughed. "I feel like a moron."

"It's okay," he said. His English wasn't bad. "There's a petrol station not far from here, but"—he eyed my flip-flops—"it's too far to walk."

Of course it was. The sun was beating down, causing the air to shimmer above the blacktop. There weren't many people around, and the few who were getting out of their cars were hurrying to the beach, completely uninterested in one lost girl and her scooter. I was on the beach, alone, with a strong-looking guy who knew I was stranded.

"You can come with me," he said once it was clear I wasn't coming up with any brilliant solutions. "My *mamma* lives nearby. We'll go there, get an extra can to hold the petrol, and then fill it up at the station and bring it back here." He looked around and nodded. "Your scooter will be safe here. I do not think anyone will hurt it."

For a moment, my heart soared with relief at his offer and then just as quickly it plummeted again. I couldn't afford to be too choosy, and I didn't exactly have a better idea, but it seemed like a bad idea to go off with a near stranger who knew exactly how helpless and friendless I was. AFN commercials were dancing in my head.

He seemed like a decent guy, but I'd only met him five minutes ago. He could take me anywhere, do anything. He *seemed* like a nice guy, but just because a guy listens to a sob story and offers to help didn't make him safe. Whether I'd be safer trying to hike it to the gas station alone was debatable, but going with him would violate every cliché of commonsense safety I'd ever learned.

"I'm sorry," I said. "Thank you so much, but . . ." I paused, not sure how to say this. "I don't know you. Not really. I can't go with someone I don't know." I wanted to cry again. "I'm sorry." Even when the perfect solution fell into my lap, I couldn't take it. For God's sake, what was I going to do?

He nodded. "I understand. This is very smart for you. But here we have a problem, no? I cannot leave you here like this. This is very bad." He thought for a moment, pulling at the short hairs on his chin. Suddenly he grinned. "I have an idea." He reached behind him and pulled out a slim cell phone. "Here," he said, dialing. "I will call *mia mamma*; she will tell you that you can trust me. That I am not *pazzo*." He circled his finger by his temple. "Not crazy."

I opened my mouth to say something but couldn't think of anything to say. I heard him say, *"Ciao, Mamma,"* and a stream of rapid Italian followed. The next thing I knew, he handed me the phone. Not knowing what else to do, I took it from him and held it to my ear.

"Hello?" I said.

"Pronto," an older woman's voice said. "You are the girl with the scooter problems that my boy wants to bring home, *sì*?"

"Yes," I said. *"Sì."*

"He is a good boy. He is always helping. He will drive you straight here and we will eat together."

"Uh."

"You do not need to worry. He is *simpatico*. In English, I do not know how you say this. But it is very good."

She talked in a rapid stream of English and Italian with such a thick accent that I couldn't tell which was which half the time. I had the impression that on her end of the line, she was using her hands as she talked. She promised me a hot meal and ceaselessly praised her son. Finally, more to get her to stop than anything else, I said, "Okay. I'll come. Thank you very much, ma'am. I'll see you soon." I handed him back the phone; he talked for another few moments with his mother and hung up.

"She said I must give you a helmet," he said. We walked over to the road where his little white scooter was parked. He unlocked the tiny compartment behind his seat and pulled out a white helmet that looked like a giant egg. I put it on. He grinned at me. He pulled on his helmet, which was a much classier dark gray.

"*Bene*, now come. *Mia mamma* is expecting us." I swung a leg over the Vespa, settled down in the seat, and held on to the small handles on either side of me. His vehicle was larger and more powerful than my cheap little scooter.

"Okay," I said, gulping. Sitting behing him, his broad back blocking my view, I felt like I would fall off. "I'm ready."

We roared along the busy road, by all those summer people heading to the beach or coming home to shower, deciding where to go out to eat or what to cook for dinner.

We left the road near the public beach, and he drove to a quiet neighborhood with beautiful, large homes. He stopped in front of a fairly large house with pale yellow terra-cotta walls and a circular drive.

"Wait," I said. "I don't even know your name."

"I'm Paolo," he said. "Now come. My *mamma* doesn't bite."

We walked through a narrow walkway I wanted to look at more closely—there was a geometric mosaic on the floor—but Paolo was already past it, heading toward the large glass doors on the opposite end. I hurried after him, throwing a last, quick look behind my shoulder as we left. We entered the main part of the house. It had a marble floor, and the walls were a shiny pale salmon. That was all I had time to notice before we were through that room and into the next, a smaller, cozier room with a tall bookcase and several love seats in beige and green. He looked around, clearly expecting to see someone, then shouted, "*Mamma, siamo qui.*"

A short, plump woman came bustling through the door, wiping her hands on her apron. She smiled broadly when she saw me and hurried over.

"Che piccolina," she said. She stroked my cheek and my hair. Her hands were soft with short broad fingers that smelled of garlic. I was surprised at her touch, her warmth. I'd pictured someone tall and aloof living in a place like this, all silver hair and Hermès silk scarves, but this woman had dark hair in a low bun and wore rubber house shoes. There was an unmistakable shadow of a mustache over her lip.

And then it clicked. Because while Paolo had changed quite a lot from when he was ten, his mother had not.

"Oh my gosh," I said, feeling a blooming happiness, a sudden sense of a small universe that occasionally could surprise you with a happy ending. "I'm Arden Vogel. Do you remember me?"

21.

"Arden?" Paolo said as it slowly dawned on him who I was. "*Mamma*, do you remember who this is?"

Her welcoming smile grew even bigger and her face glowed as she cupped my face, studying the changes. She was quite a bit shorter than me.

"Arden," she crooned, opening her arms. "*Che piccollna. Che bella.*"

I launched myself at her and she held me. She was soft and warm and smelled of suntan oil, garlic, and basil. I wanted to crawl into her, I wanted to escape, to go back in time to when I was little and everything turned out all right.

After minutes passed, I released her and she looked up at my face and stroked my cheek.

"*Bella,*" she said. "*Che bella.*"

I wiped my eyes and we all laughed as she did the same.

"I can't believe this," I said. "After all this time. I found you again."

"No," Paolo said. "I found you again!"

We laughed once more and our laughter brought people from the kitchen to come see what the commotion was about. Soon the living room was full of people all exclaiming loudly in Italian, trying to pry the story out, remembering me as a little child and touching my long curly hair in bemusement.

Paolo's mother grabbed my hand and pulled me along to the kitchen even though I was in the middle of talking to Paolo's father. She sat down at the long kitchen table and set a glass of sparkling water in front of me.

In my broken Italian, to a rapt audience of five adults, I gave a brief synopsis of the past ten years. When I told them my father had died, they all grew quiet and solemn. It almost undid me, but I continued. I told them that I was in college now, that I was here to close up the house. I told them my mother was in Iraq.

It was surreal to be there, sitting with Paolo by my side and his mother holding my hand, stroking it. I wanted to laugh and to cry because I thought everything was lost and all I had were memories, but here they were, Paolo and his mother, older and real. I wasn't finished making happy memories in Sardinia.

"I remember you so well," Paolo said. "You had a striped pink and red bathing suit, so different from anything Italian girls were wearing. You had pale skin, blotched pink like your suit from crying so hard at the water's edge. I wanted to take care of you, this foreign girl."

It was the first time I'd heard our meeting from his point of view.

As we continued to marvel at the strangeness of life, the mysteries of reunions, and how small the world was, a shadow crossed in front of me. Paolo's mother looked and smiled at a girl biting into a peach.

"You're awake, *cara*. Come meet our visitor!"

"*Dio*," the stranger said breathlessly. "I slept for so long!"

I looked to see a hugely pregnant girl ease her way down to the chair Paolo held out for her.

"Arden," Paolo said. "This is my wife, Anna. Anna, this is Arden, who we knew a long time ago, when we were children."

Anna reached out a warm, sticky hand and we shook.

I tried not to show how shocked I was, but I'm sure I failed. Paolo was twenty years old. He was married with a pregnant wife?

Anna had light brown hair with pale skin that nearly glowed against her black maternity bathing suit.

Paolo had rescued another girl. I wondered if the baby was his. The thought was unkind, but it felt true.

It saddened me to think I was the first in a line of rescues, but then I did need rescuing when I was five. I was nineteen now, and barring a couple of small exceptions, I could rescue myself. So that was something.

"*Piacere*," Anna said.

I smiled back.

In the end, when I told them I was staying at the house alone, they insisted I move in with them.

"I need to go through the house," I said halfheartedly. "To get it ready for the sale." Staying at Paolo's sounded much better. Between his mom's cooking, the company, and that wonderful feeling of being around people from my past, going to my old cabin didn't hold much appeal.

"Stay here with us," Paolo said. "You can go back to your house later. How long does it take?"

"I wouldn't want to get in your way."

Paolo's mother gasped in mock outrage when Paolo translated. She said something in quick, furious Italian, pointing at me, at herself, at the ceiling, and for some reason also at a bowl of peaches on the table. I pretended to shrink back in my seat and everyone laughed.

"Sorry, *bella*," Paolo said, grinning. "When *mia mamma* decides something, it is the law. You understand?"

"Yeah," I said, smiling back. "Okay. I'll stay with you guys. Thanks."

Was it cowardly to dodge staying at the house? Maybe. Although it felt right. This was about looking forward, about making friends, not about running away.

After I told my story, they told me theirs. It turned out they had sold the house they used to vacation in all those years ago. Paolo's dad had lost his job and they needed the money. They didn't return to Sardinia for many years. In fact, this was their first time back. They finally had the money to buy a house, and we all agreed it was more beautiful than their old place. When they showed me to my room, I saw that it was airy with cool white walls and a bright blue bedspread, echoing the colors of my mother's ceramic plates. With the window open, I could both hear the ocean and smell the salt on the breeze.

Even though my Italian wasn't great, and with the exception of Paolo, they hardly spoke any English, I felt welcomed and at ease.

I couldn't always blend in. But I was beginning to see that being a human chameleon wasn't necessarily a good way to go through life.

22.

Paolo had a computer with an Internet connection at his house. The next morning, while the rest of the family went to church, I logged on to discover the damage my e-mails from the day before had caused. I clicked open my mom's e-mail with dread instead of the usual relief I felt at seeing a message from her.

But perhaps as I had done from the very beginning, I had underestimated and misunderstood her.

Arden, she wrote, and I could almost hear the mix of exasperation and love, *I miss you too, baby. I know it isn't easy for you.*

I don't know where you got the idea that I didn't know you missed me or were scared for me. I'm scared too, honey. Not just for me. I'm scared for you. You're traveling alone in Europe; you think a mother doesn't worry about a child who does that? What if you get stranded somewhere?

I wanted to laugh.

I didn't tell you not to go, I didn't even tell you how much you scare me sometimes with the choices you make, because you need to have adventures, meet new friends, experience the world.

It's all part of life, sweetheart. Having adventures, traveling, eating good food, exploring. And loving people and being scared for them. It's all normal.

I know that you love me. I don't know if you can know how much I love you.

Mom

She was right, and it seemed so obvious now. Who did I think I was fooling? Why did I try to pretend I wasn't scared or lonely without her nearby? The simple acknowledgment of the normalcy of those feelings helped alleviate them.

Smiling, I wrote her back. Telling her all about Paolo and his family (leaving out the part about the empty tank of gas because really, my mother didn't need to hear how stupid her daughter could be sometimes). But this time, I didn't have the feeling that she couldn't handle the truth. I knew she could.

There was no message from Peter.

The next morning, I drove my scooter, its tank full, down to the shore so early that there weren't other bathers yet. Everyone else at the house was still sleeping. Low, heavy clouds made everything bright and hazy at the same time. The air was thick and moist and felt like rain. Sardinia was mostly desert with an average of three rainy days each summer. Today, it seemed, would be one of them. The normally bright blue water had taken on the same subdued gray shades of the sky. There were almost no waves; the water looked smooth and flat enough to walk on. The horizon melted so that I couldn't tell, though I stared hard, where the sea ended and the sky began. It was a flat silver disk that extended in all directions, in front of me, above me, all around.

Whether it was the early hour, barely seven, or the heavy clouds, the normal noises I expected to hear at the beach were gone. Muted. The gulls didn't cry. The lap of the tiny waves on the sand was faint.

I shoved my hands in my pockets and found a large flat rock to sit on.

I had felt abandoned for so long, but when I looked back, I finally saw that I had done a lot of leaving myself. I was the one who had walked away from Peter two years ago, the one who walked away from the Texans. I never tried to make my friendships work because I knew I would leave them in the near future. But I wasn't a child anymore; I wasn't bound by military moves. I had three years left in Nashville and I'd never lived anywhere four years in a row. It was a new chance to make friends and keep them. A new chance to put down roots and see if I liked it.

The water was so calm, I could hardly see any ripples out past the shore. The few seabirds floating were barely bobbing.

Please write me back, Peter.

I searched for dolphins, for black fins cutting the water. An up-down movement meant the dorsal fin belonged to a dolphin. A triangular dorsal that zigzagged from side to side meant there was a shark in the water.

If I see a dolphin, then Peter will write back that he likes me, I decided half seriously. If I see a shark, then it means he won't.

I didn't see either.

By the time I made it back to the house, I found the place bustling.

"Arden," Paolo said. "We are going to visit my *nonna*. Will you come?"

"Of course," I said. "Yes."

"Not everyone has met Anna yet," Paolo explained as I

helped him pack the car. "Many of my relatives from all over Italy are coming this week. We are all meeting in Alghero, near the Grotta di Nettuno. You know?"

I did know Neptune's Grotto, long, snaking caves filled with incredible stalactites and stalagmites. My father and I had visited them years ago, taking a boat to get there, leaving my mother to shop in Alghero in peace.

I helped Paolo load dish after covered dish in the small truck, some wrapped in towels to keep hot, some in zippered insulated coolers to stay cold.

"When did your mother cook all this?" I asked. "No one was up this morning."

Paolo shrugged, immune to the kitchen magic his mother wielded.

Right before we all clambered in the tiny two-door, Paolo's mother handed Anna and me each a thick slice of buttered toast, sprinkled with sugar.

"*Mangiate*," she commanded. Eat.

Anna and I shared a smile. What was Anna's background that she soaked up the fussing, the nurturing, the feeding as happily as I did?

I bit into the sweet, buttery toast, the sugar crunching pleasantly, and thought back to my long-ago visit to the grotto.

There were stalagmites shaped like popes and wicked witches, stalagmites that looked like warriors and organ pipes. Throughout the caves, there was an eerie, phosphorescent glow.

My dad, who had read up on the caves, pointed out something green spreading on the thick columns.

"That's mold," he had whispered to me. "From the lighting system. This cave is not meant for light. It's supposed to be dark in here."

I slipped my hand into his and we continued on in the artificial light, seeing things we weren't meant to see.

The park where the reunion took place was teeming with people. It took me a moment to realize they were all Paolo's relatives. Long tables had been put up and women busily set out food. There were blankets on the grass full of people lounging and playing with toddlers, and several groups of men and boys kicked a soccer ball.

There were no chairs except for one under the shade of a large tree. A short, heavy woman sat there. She wore black and had thin hair, dyed brown, styled in a short bouffant. Various people brought her tidbits on small plates, like offerings to a queen.

"That is Nonna," Paolo said for my benefit and Anna's.

He took Anna's hand, and with me following, we approached her folding chair.

As we drew closer, I realized she was much older than I'd first thought. In her nineties, at least. Her small face had somewhat crumpled in on itself. Her lips curled in and her eyes peered under folds of skin. Her skin looked thin and yellow, like parchment, and I could see her scalp through the thin hair.

Crouching in front of this living ancestor, Paolo laid a soft hand on her knee.

"Nonna," he said. "*Questa è Anna.*"

"Anna." Her face broke out in a smile, her eyes disappearing altogether. "*Vieni, vieni.*" She motioned with her hands toward her, and Anna knelt at her feet. Nonna placed a hand, fingers thick and curled from arthritis, on Anna's golden hair. It looked like a benediction. Maybe it was. Anna closed her eyes for a moment, then opened them and smiled at her.

"*Piacere,*" she said, and leaned up to kiss her cheek.

Then Anna struggled to her feet with her heavy belly and someone nudged me toward Nonna.

"Nonna," Paolo said again. "*Questa è* Arden."

Someone must have filled her in on who I was because she didn't hesitate.

"Arden," she said, smiling at me as well. "*Vieni, vieni.*"

Following Anna's example, I stepped forward and knelt in front of her. I realized it must help her see the person she was talking to. She laid a soft, warm hand on my shoulder and then slid it to the side of my face, cupping my cheeks.

For some reason, I felt like crying.

"Sha, sha, sha," she soothed, feeling the sudden heat in my cheeks, the thick swallowing to hold back tears. She said something in Italian, but I couldn't catch the words. Someone touched my shoulder and I realized my turn was over.

I stood up and walked over to where Anna's and Paolo's parents were. Paolo stayed at Nonna's feet and I heard soft murmuring between the two of them. After a few moments, he joined us.

"Paolo," I said. "What did she say to me?" I should have understood it, but she mumbled her words and her accent was strange.

He smiled and looked both sad and calm. "She said, 'Everything will be all right.' She tells everybody that."

Then Paolo stepped toward Anna and she laid her head on his shoulder. They shared a look, something private, tender. He softly patted her tight round tummy, and then with an arm around her, he walked with her toward the table with food. I thought of Madison. I suddenly felt very sorry for her that she was going through her pregnancy alone. And then I realized that Madison wasn't alone. She had Katie and Lola and they were doing their best, just as Paolo was doing his best for Anna.

I wished that I could tell them I was sorry. I dropped my hands to my sides and shrugged to no one in particular.

"*Vieni*, Arden," I heard someone call to me. Come, eat.

I hurried toward the food, the smells of oregano, melted cheese, warm bread filling the air. I smiled for these new friends and vowed to be a better friend in the future.

It took two agonizing days.

I received regular e-mails from my mom. More about the ridiculous heat, a bit about a coworker with a family emergency back home. No heavy casualties, thank goodness. And no message from Peter.

When I opened my account and finally had an e-mail from him, I paused for a moment. I promised myself that no matter what he wrote, everything would be all right.

Arden, I just got back from a two-day retreat with the team.

That was why he hadn't written.

I still think about graduation night too, he wrote. *I used to wonder if I'd made the biggest mistake of my life, kissing you. Even though it's one of the best memories I have. When you stopped me, my heart almost stopped. I hated myself for making you feel even worse than you already did.*

I wanted to cry, reading that. It came close to breaking my heart, how we'd both been haunted by the same sweet moment and how I'd pushed it away.

I would really like to try kissing you again.

My face grew hot. The vivid image of our next kiss made my toes curl against the cool tile floor. I couldn't stop a silly grin. Peter liked me.

I still didn't know how we'd make it work, living so far apart, but at least now we both knew how we felt, and that felt wonderful.

23.

On my fifth day with Paolo's family, I decided to go to the house and walk through it one last time. I needed to throw away the food I'd bought and to pick up the few things I was going to keep. The time spent with Paolo's family had done a lot to help me see that Sardinia was still a haven and always would be, no matter whether we owned a house here or not. I wasn't as scared or depressed about saying goodbye, though it wasn't anything I was looking forward to. Paolo and Anna offered to come and keep me company, but I told them I needed to do this alone.

I parked my scooter by the kitchen door and took out my key, knowing that this would be the last time I ever used it to open the house. I took a deep breath and reminded myself that nothing in life was permanent.

The house felt unused and unlived in. I told it not to worry, a new family was coming and they would love it as much as we had loved it.

The downstairs was stuffy, so I opened the windows to air it out one last time. I collected all the food and perishables and threw them away in the trash can outside. Opened drawers and cabinets to see what I wanted to keep.

A car door slammed outside.

My take-home pile was still small. The ceramic plates, the plastic ladle and mug, several of the CDs, and the dark blue curtains that hung over my bedroom window. Maybe I would turn them into a pillow. Or maybe I'd hang them over my window at school, a bit of Sardinia and childhood to keep.

I touched the windowpane, ran a hand along my stripped bed, and told the place goodbye.

I was back downstairs, wrapping the plates in newspaper to protect them on the flights back, when I stopped. The voices that I'd heard and assumed belonged to some neighbors or guests had gotten louder. They were speaking in English with a distinct Texan accent.

I put down the half-wrapped plates and rushed outside.

"Don't think it was easy to find you," Madison said as soon as she saw me, hands on her hips.

I stood there dumbfounded.

"Seriously, we could become travel guides," she said, trying not to grin but failing. "We could open an agency."

"That would be so awesome," Lola said. They high-fived. Katie was by their bags, grinning broadly and looking pleased with herself.

"I can't believe this," I said. "I mean, how did you . . . what . . . I mean . . . I—" I looked over at Katie for an explanation.

"We didn't want to leave you on such a bad note," she said. "You were the highlight of our European vacation. You left the address, so we figured, why not?"

"You talked about the house in Sardinia so much, it sounded great. And since we didn't have firm plans for the trip, we just changed our itinerary," Madison said. "Although getting to this island wasn't as easy as you made it sound." She took in my astonished look. "You think we're nuts, don't you?"

"No, I didn't mean—" *They came back,* I kept thinking, *they actually came to find me.* No one had ever done that for me.

"You do," she said. "You know it."

"Maybe I do." I felt myself grinning, bursting with sudden joy. "You *are* nuts."

"It's true," Lola said. "We all are."

She stepped forward and grabbed my hand. I squeezed and she did too. Madison and Katie each put a hand on my shoulder.

"You guys are awesome," I said.

"Don't mess with Texas," Katie said lightly. "We'll come after you and hunt you down."

It took a while to get the full story out. We went to the café down the street and we all ordered cold coffee, which in Italy meant a tall glass of lukewarm coffee with a single ice cube bobbing on the top. Roberto and his wife fussed over us and insisted on bringing the drinks to our seats instead of letting us carry them ourselves. I noticed, however, that they didn't protest when we paid. Life was returning to normal.

"We couldn't believe when we came back and you'd left, Arden," Madison said. "We were so upset."

"I'm sorry," I said, feeling the size of an ant. "I didn't know what to do. I mean, you guys are such good friends, I felt like this fourth wheel. And then Lola and I had a fight and I figured it'd be easiest if I left."

"Haven't you ever been in a fight before?" Lola asked, hurt and surprised. "You don't just walk away like that."

"I'm sorry," I said again. "I'm really glad you guys came. I can't tell you how many times I've thought of you. I wanted to go back and apologize, but it was too late. I was already here and I knew you'd be long gone. It's like you said, Lola," I teased. "No one's perfect. Not even me."

"Definitely not you," she shot back.

"You did leave us the address," Madison said. "That redeems you a bit."

"How are you feeling?" I said.

"Better." Her hand went automatically to her stomach, and from the protectiveness of the gesture I knew she was keeping the baby. "I mean, the hunger comes and goes and I puked a lot on the ferry, but I don't know if that's morning sickness or seasickness."

She reached out for my hand and I held it, her hand tiny in mine.

"I'm lucky that I have choices," she said simply. "It makes it easier. I know that it's my decision. And I'm keeping her. Or him."

"You're going to be an awesome mom," I said. "I can tell these things."

"I'm glad you mentioned that," Lola said. "We've been thinking."

"Yeah?"

"Why don't you transfer to UT?" Madison blurted out. "I mean, what's so great about Vanderbilt? Austin is awesome."

"It really is," Lola said. "And if you transfer, you'll be closer to that guy you like; what's his name?"

"Peter," I said, feeling a blush just saying his name.

"You can help me with this baby because I'm not moving

home and I'm not dropping out," Madison said with a mix of bravado and fear.

"And we can help you," Katie said.

It was such a lovely thing to say and exactly what I needed to hear. It was an impulsive, generous gesture, like inviting me to join them on the trip in the first place. I didn't know what to say. Then I realized that I did. I smiled at them because they were sweet to come find me, to invite me to join them at school. They were wonderful people and I could finally admit to myself that I cared for them a lot.

But I said no. It wasn't the right decision to make. There are times when you don't jump.

"We'll always have Paris," I told them. They laughed, like I knew they would.

I moved back to my house with the Texans. There was no room for the four of us in Paolo's house. This time, when I lay in bed, my fingertips on the windowpane, I didn't imagine my parents' murmur. I heard Lola and Madison giggling downstairs. Katie was in my room and we stayed up late, talking about the latest developments with Peter, about my mom, my dad, and her family.

"When I was a kid, I always felt control was key," Katie said. "After my mom left, the house was a disaster. My father let everything fall apart. It took months before he could bring himself to take the trash out, to cook a meal, to do the dishes. It's probably why I'm so anal about these things now. I have this terrible fear of the unknown, of new places, of strangers."

"But you're an amazing traveler. You have everything together."

"That's not an accident. I have it like that or I freak. That's why I wanted Lola with me. I know she upset you, but she knows how to enjoy herself. She's like the Cat in the Hat, and I'm the scolding fish."

I laughed, but I realized that I had seen a different side of Lola. I saw the side that was afraid and that hid the fear behind a great big laugh. She gave away pieces of herself too easily. She even left her possessions strewn behind like a series of bread-crumbs marking a trail. But it wasn't my place to pull aside the curtain.

"That is a wonderful thing about Lola," I said. "It's something I need to get better at too."

I took them to the agency the next morning and we rented scooters for all. I showed them the basics, and before long, we were all zooming along like a motorcycle gang. A cute one. On scooters.

I showed them the fancy Costa Smeralda, the emerald coast, where the millionaires docked their yachts. We gaped at the ridiculously priced items in the stores, admired the beautiful women on the arms of tanned, powerful-looking men, and invented stories for how they met.

"The lounge at the Concord," Madison suggested.

"No way. They both wanted the same taxi, and in the end, they shared a ride and a whole lot more . . . ," Lola said. "Hubba, hubba."

"That was a movie, you idiot," Madison said.

"The personal ads," I said. "They met on the Internet."

"If that's the type of people who are looking for love online, I've got to start logging on more often," Lola said.

We laughed loudly and a handsome couple looked over their shoulders at us.

Lola waved and they nodded back.

From there, we went to the Costa Verde, the green coast, for a less opulent, more down-to-earth version of stunning views and a beautiful coastline.

We had a meal on the beach with the traditional flat crunchy bread known as *carta da musica*, music paper, because it's so thin, and we spread it with a local cream cheese. The cheese was called *casu marzu*. I waited until they'd all had a few bites and agreed it was delicious before I told them *casu marzu* means rotten cheese.

"That's odd," Katie said. "Why do they call it that? It's not rotten."

"Well . . . ," I said. Everyone's eyes grew large.

"Arden, what the hell have you been feeding us?" Lola asked.

I started to laugh. "The way they make this cheese," I said between snorts and gasps at their identical horrified expressions, "is they take a block of cheese and cut a hole in it. They pour olive oil into the hole and then wait."

"Why?" The word was suspicious, the gleam in their eyes murderous.

"They wait for a special fly, the cheese fly, to come and leave behind its larvae."

"As in maggots?" Madison shrieked. "I'm pregnant, I can't eat maggots."

"The little suckers eat the cheese and wiggle around so much that it turns it nice and creamy," I said happily.

"Arden, I'm going to kill you," Madison said. "Please tell me you're joking."

"Nope. But you said so yourself—the cheese is delicious. I think your words were, 'Mmm. This is so good. There's something different about it, it's so creamy and smooth.'"

I got a fistful of sand pelted in my face.

* * *

Later, when we were down at the beach and Lola and Madison were splashing in the tide, Katie turned to me and invited me again. Katie-style, her invitation was full of practical points selling UT over Vanderbilt.

"It would be a big change," she said in the end. "But the house we're renting next year has an extra room, and I know we'd get along as roommates."

We exchanged a smile.

"I'll think about it," I promised. "But this isn't one of those snap decisions." The sun was low and heavy on the horizon, tinting the sky and the sea a soft purple-peach.

"I know it isn't," she said, and we both turned back to face the water. "I'd feel the same."

"Look, you guys," Madison called out, and pointed. "Dolphins!"

Three small dorsal fins curved out of the water and slipped back under again. Then two more glided up and down. The water had turned a soft lilac, and the dolphins looked like they were swimming in melted watercolors.

For once, I simply stood there at the edge and enjoyed the view.

Six Months Later

I'm standing with all the other family members by the huge glass windows overlooking the tarmac. People have made banners saying WELCOME HOME! and WE LOVE YOU, BAGH-DADDY! It's freezing outside, and everyone has stripped off the heavy coats they came here with; small islands of Gore-Tex and wool surround them. Some people have been here for hours; they've brought coolers with soda and food. The atmosphere is one of giddy anticipation laced with anxiety. Even though we're all counting down the minutes, everyone knows there could be delays. Rumors rush forward and back through the crowd. A second deployment will be announced in three months. Everyone's leave is canceled. The plane will be late because of mechanical difficulties in Kuwait.

I don't know where people are getting these rumors. I try to ignore them.

Then there's a gasp and we all turn to stare with hunger and joy at the large green-gray C-5 plane coming in for a landing. As it lands, everyone starts cheering and clapping and hugging one another. They're home. Our soldiers are home. Some people are already crying.

It takes forever and we're all out of patience waiting for the soldiers to come through the doors. We're in a huge waiting area and it's too small to contain all the emotions. Now that they're here, now that they've landed, we want them. We can't wait a minute longer. But we do.

Then the doors swing open and they start coming through, huge grins on their tanned faces. The families are going crazy. I'm surrounded by shouts of "Daddy! Daddy!"

A little six-year-old has wrapped her arms around a soldier's legs and is sobbing.

My eyes swim and for a second all the soldiers walking toward us blur into a smear of sandy brown.

They look the same. They look tired.

Then one face stands out clearly and I see her.

"Mom!" I shout, jumping up and down, waving my arms. "Mom!"

She scans the crowd and then she sees me.

She drops her rucksack and I run toward her, cutting through the crowd, the people hugging and the people still searching. I push past them and I fly into her arms and she hugs me. She smells different, of sharp things, sweat, and plane fumes, but under that it's her smell and I dig my nose into the crook of her neck and she yelps.

"I'm so glad," I say. I can't think straight. It's all I can say. "I'm so glad you're back."

"Me too, baby. Me too."

I let her go and look behind me. Peter is there, easy to find, taller than everyone else. He's been standing to the side, waiting for the hugs to finish. I reach out my hand for him and feel his large warm palm clasp mine. He came with me to Germany, missing a week of swimming practice, so I wouldn't have to wait for my mom alone. Katie offered to come as well. We keep in touch through e-mail, but I told her to save those frequent-flier miles and to come visit me at Vanderbilt over spring break instead.

My mom hugs Peter and kisses him on the cheek. He has to bend down for her to reach him.

"Peter," she says. "It's been a while. It's good to see you."

"Ditto, Colonel Vogel," he says, smiling. "Welcome back."

It's perfect.

She's home safe. And so am I.

Acknowledgments

I have never served in a war, and I have never been a soldier. But I was five years old when my father was called off the reserves to go fight in Lebanon. And I was twenty-five when my husband was deployed to serve in Central America.

While I use my imagination to put myself in the dusty boots of a soldier at war, I need only use my memories to know what it's like to be a family member left behind, waiting for news from a loved one.

The soldiers who have served or are currently serving in Iraq are making a huge sacrifice. They are brave, loyal, and strong. But they leave behind brave, loyal, and strong wives and husbands, children and parents, who are forced to let their beloveds go in harm's way.

Newborns learn to walk before they ever meet their fathers. Wives and husbands communicate with e-mail and snatched conversations from worlds apart. No matter how full your days are, the nights are long and lonely. You watch the news with seething frustration when the lead story is about a singing cat instead of the unit you need to know about. You live in a parallel universe—physically, you're safe; emotionally, you're trying to weather a hurricane.

This is the heartache en masse that doesn't appear on the TV or in the papers. But make no mistake, the pain and longing at home is a terrible price hundreds of thousands of Americans pay whenever we go to war. I can't erase that pain, but I can bear witness.

Thank you to Sergeant First Class Elle Whitacre, Lieutenant Colonel Michael Jaffee, Colonel Fred Taylor, and the other men and women serving our country who took the time to describe to me what deployed life is like. Thank you for sharing the painful, funny, intense memories from your time in Iraq. You have been shot at, have lost friends, and have been apart from your families during critical life events. You have worked long days and longer nights. You have done this because you believe in our country and in the service members you fight with. Thank you.

Bonnie Taylor—I still owe you fruit tea and spinach crescents for all your help and insights. You make homeschooling two kids in Germany while your husband is deployed look easy.

Michelle Koidin Jaffee—who wrote a column for the *San Antonio Express-News* called "Double Duty," describing her experiences raising newborn twins while her husband was deployed. Thank you for helping me with the technical details of how families keep in touch. Technology is a wonderful thing.

Leah Corsover, Kerri Sarembock, Denise Grolly-Case—for sharing diaries and experiences as young women traveling in foreign lands.

Andrea Marasco—who first introduced me to Sardinia and whose family has come to define warm hospitality and good food.

David Liss, Billy Taylor—fellow writers and readers of early drafts. Their talent is only matched by their tact.

Ben Possick—swim expert extraordinaire.

Captain Mason Weiss—who introduced me to Admiral Stockdale and the Stoic philosophy.

Dan Laufer and Molly Harris—who did their best to keep me up to date on college trends. Rainbows are really expensive flip-flops, if anyone was wondering.

Erin Clarke—my fantastic, very patient, talented editor. Thank you for everything. Most writers only dream of having such a clear-sighted, thoughtful editor, but I actually have one.

Stephen Barbara—my agent, who believed in this book (and in me) and championed both of us.

My family, who stopped strangers on the street to tell them about my book. I love you guys.

And finally, I can't thank the two most important men in my life enough: Fred and Tovar. You make everything better.